BOOK CLUB BAIT & SWITCH

A SHELF INDULGENCE COZY MYSTERY

S.E. BABIN

All rights reserved.

No part of this publication may be sold, copied, distributed, reproduced or transmitted in any form or by any means, mechanical or digital, including photocopying and recording or by any information storage and retrieval system without the prior written permission of both the publisher, Oliver Heber Books and the author, S.E. Babin, except in the case of brief quotations embodied in critical articles and reviews.

PUBLISHER'S NOTE: This is a work of fiction. Names, characters, places, and incidents either are the product of the author's imagination or are used fictitiously. Any resemblance to actual persons, living or dead, business establishments, events, or locales is entirely coincidental.

Book Club Bait & Switch Copyright 2025 © S.E. Babin

Cover art by Lou Harper from Cover Affairs

Published by Oliver-Heber Books

0 9 8 7 6 5 4 3 2 1

ONE

Snow drifted from the sky, fresh and undisturbed as it stuck to the quiet winter streets. Poppy loudly yowled her displeasure as I lifted her from the toasty warmth of the car and into the frigid morning air. I wrapped my oversized scarf around her and held her close for the short walk into the shop.

"Relax," I muttered into the ruff of her neck as she tried to burrow inside me to warm herself. "You have fur."

She jumped out of my arms the second the shop door closed behind us, heading straight for the small heater Harper kept by the register to keep her feet warm.

"High maintenance little thing," I said with a sigh and bent to turn it on before setting all my stuff down on the counter.

Christmas was right around the corner, bringing with it the fresh scent of winter in the air and a sense of renewal as we approached a new year. For me, it brought new happiness but also quite a bit of stress. Planning a wedding during the holidays was not for the faint of heart.

We thought about getting married right away, but we had Izzy, Hardy's daughter, to think about. She'd gone through a lot over the last eighteen months, and a quick marriage seemed unwise given everything that had happened. So Hardy and I decided to wait and take things slowly.

A little over a year later, our wedding approached with the speed of a bullet train. I'd slowly been planning the day with Harper and Fletcher's help. It wouldn't be an elaborate affair, but it would be a day to share with our friends and family, containing a mix of things Hardy and I loved.

The thought made me smile. It took a lot of work on our part to make our relationship successful, especially with my chosen career path and Izzy's sudden arrival in his life. But that's the thing about relationships. They all take work. It's always easier to walk away, but sometimes you meet someone you don't want to live your life without.

Hardy was that person for me.

Poppy curled up into a little apostrophe, tucking her tail around her, and closed her eyes, content as the small heater worked overtime to warm the frigid shop. I'd done a lot of work to the building over the last couple of years, but every winter I made a mental note to install a fireplace, only to forget about it once warmer temperatures rolled in.

Maybe next year I'd finally buckle down and get it done. Harper would appreciate it since she was all but running the shop these days. And staring down at my lazy cat, I knew Poppy would, too.

I took a few minutes to straighten up some books and wipe down the front register area. Harper would be in soon, back from a visit to family from out of state, and I wanted to make sure she arrived back to a tidy store. I'd hired new help a few months ago after the other girls moved on to bigger and better things, and one of them wasn't working out nearly as well as the other. I tried to hire book lovers who'd been to the store and whom I was familiar with, but our town didn't have a lot of younger people looking for an entry-level job.

It didn't help that I kept getting involved in murders—on purpose now, which I'm sure hadn't endeared me to much of the community. Though the people I'd helped over the years had a different opinion, I hoped.

The second new girl was named Tiffany. She was bright but sullen, and I wasn't sure she read as much as she claimed to on her application. I'd given her the day off since Harper was back on the schedule, but I had to figure out how to let her down easily before her next work day.

Being a business owner wasn't fun sometimes. For an evil second, I thought about passing the duty to Harper before brushing it away. I hired her. I'd be the one to let her go.

Poppy rolled onto her belly and yowled at me. "Don't give me that. You're sprawled in front of the heater, all warm and snug, and I have to open the shop." Tugging my cardigan closer, I stuck my tongue out at the cat and went to start a pot of coffee.

HARPER BREEZED IN AN HOUR LATER, trailing a gust of cold air and snow behind her as she came inside. "Brr," she breathed, rubbing her hands together. Harper laughed when she spotted Poppy sprawled on her back and set her things by the register before dropping to her knees to give the cat a belly rub.

"How was your trip?" I handed her a cup of peppermint tea.

She sighed in thanks. "Wonderful. Mom loved Jack." Harper rolled her eyes. "He spent years being a grump to me, but Mom loved him in less than a minute."

Jack owned a furniture store down the road. He had quite the gift for woodworking, and every time I walked past his store, I drooled a little over his offerings. For a while, he and Harper had a rivalry going trying to win the town's window display contest. He took home the trophy most years, but last year, Harper managed to beat him. It sparked something between them, and they'd been dating for the last six months.

I liked Jack, but I wondered if he was the right guy for her. In about ten minutes, the guy I thought might be better for her would come into the shop, antagonize her, and head into the back part of Tattered Pages to help dole out the cases for the week.

Quinn Bryant, a former FBI agent, had come to work

for us after we'd partnered on a case together. He and Hardy had become fast friends. It'd taken us a while to get on friendly terms. Even now, we bickered like siblings.

He'd lost his wife some time back and had grieved for a long time. Even now, he'd suddenly get a soft look in his eyes, and he'd stare outside for a while before shaking it off and getting back to work.

He seemed smitten by Harper, but had backed off when she started dating Jack.

I didn't dislike Jack, but he had a way of making his barbs a little too sharp. Quinn and I may fight, but he'd never been anything less than honest with me and never purposely tried to hurt me. If Harper gave him a chance, she might fall head over heels.

I frowned. Now that I'd had the thought, I wondered if that was exactly the reason why Harper hadn't given him the time of day. A chemistry lingered between them, but Quinn respected her boundaries, and Harper never stepped an inch over the line.

It was maddening. And also, none of my business. Harper was an adult and would figure it out.

"I'm glad you had a good trip. Get settled in, and I'll catch you up on everything that happened while you were gone."

She gave me a sharp glance at my tone, but I smiled. "It will hold."

"Uh oh." Harper picked up her bags and rose to her feet. "Back to the grind, I guess."

I grinned. "Them's the perks of being the manager."

She rolled her eyes but laughed. "I'll be right back."

Quinn came through the door a few seconds later. "I don't think I'll ever get used to the winter around here. One minute it's 40, the next it's snowing." He stomped his boots on the rubber mat and rubbed a hand through his hair. Bright eyes swept the shop for anything out of place, a fallback gesture I suspected came from his time as an agent.

"Layers are the key." Poppy gave him the hairy eyeball as he set his beat-up leather satchel down and shrugged his jacket off. She liked Quinn, but he'd held the door open a hair too long for her liking and now she'd hold a grudge the rest of the day.

He spotted the cat, grinned, and bent down to give her a head rub before straightening and making a beeline for the coffee pot.

Harper returned right then and stopped in her tracks, a blush coloring her cheeks. "Oh! Quinn. Hello."

"Hello, Harper." He watched her, eyes drinking her in as he poured a touch of cream into his coffee and stirred, all without looking away. I would have spilled it twice by now. Pressing my lips together to keep from smiling, I turned and went behind the register.

They'd quit making googly eyes at each other in a moment. Maybe one day, those two crazy kids would realize they were meant to be together.

Until then, I'd keep my mouth shut.

Easier said than done when you were as nosy as I happen to be.

TWO

Exhaustion pulled at my very bones. Fletcher and Harper lay sprawled on my living room floor, dozens of different types of faux flowers scattered around them. I sat cross-legged and stared in dismay at the display.

"I—"

"She's speechless," Fletcher drawled.

"Too many colors? Types? Combos?" Harper probed.

I rubbed a hand over my face.

"Too many everything," Fletcher said. She came to her feet in a single liquid motion and snatched my wine glass from the coffee table. "More wine will help."

I whimpered.

Harper sighed. "I know how much you hate this, but it's almost over. You're at the finish line."

"I just want to marry Hardy," I groaned.

Her face softened. "And you will. You have to get through all the other stuff first."

Fletcher shoved a glass of wine under my nose.

"Here. Get that one down, and I bet you'll have a change of tune."

Harper sent her an admonishing look. Fletcher winked and gave her an evil grin.

"Where's Hardy?" Fletcher asked.

"Working on a case with Quinn. Something with insurance fraud."

Fletcher's face grew curious. "Oh? Something I should know about?"

I laughed. "You and Cole are incorrigible. No. It's small-time news. An employer thing."

"Things are slow right now," she admitted. "And it doesn't help with that clock app."

Harper snorted.

"What is it? The tock thing?" She waved a hand. "Whatever. All these people who want to make a name for themselves are stealing stories right under our noses."

"Maybe you should up your social media game," Harper suggested.

Fletcher's lips curled in distaste. "And maybe people should put down their phones and pick up a newsletter or magazine every once in a while."

I snickered. "You sound eighty years old."

She groaned dramatically. "Have you ever seen the thing? All those buttons and sounds and emojis?" Fletcher rolled her eyes. "You can't even post a video without going through an entire library of music, and you gotta pick the

BOOK CLUB BAIT & SWITCH   9

one that will get the most views because people have the attention span of a drunk gnat! It's maddening."

Her flaming red hair was definitely matching her temperament this evening. I commiserated with her. Social media was exhausting, but it was a necessary evil.

"Good writing should surpass flashy videos," she grumbled, falling silent when Harper and I stared at her.

"Maybe in a certain age group," Harper conceded. "But if you're trying to reach a wider audience, you have to get creative."

"How did we turn this thing to me?" Fletcher said. "Dakota still hasn't picked out flowers."

And just like that, I was the one under the microscope again.

Forty-five minutes later, my brain was mush, but I'd made all the selections. As I was about to stand up and stretch, a fuzz ball shot out from the kitchen and launched itself at me.

I caught the cat with a deft hand. "Hey, wretch," I said to the newest addition to the family. We adopted Fang as a kitten to help Poppy out with her loneliness. His personality was the complete opposite of our other cat. Where my Persian was a little standoffish, Fang loved or hated someone immediately. He showed that love by launching himself from any and every available surface. It quickly became a game of catch him or drop whatever you were holding.

Now, all of us had honed our reflexes so well that we

almost had a second sense when Fang was about to pop out of something random and streak toward us like a rabid bat.

Fang meowed and head-butted my chin.

"Your cat is still weird," Fletcher said and rose, her knees popping as she did.

"Yep. But he's adorable, right?" I stroked a hand down Fang's silky grey and white fur.

Harper leaned over and scratched his head. "Sure is." She stood and gathered the wine glasses while Fletcher took the wine bottle and the platter of crackers and cheese to the kitchen.

"Are there any more decisions?" I asked, unable to keep the plaintive note from my voice.

Fletcher grinned. "Some, but I think we can handle most of them." She turned on the faucet.

"Don't worry about that. I'll do them later."

"Nonsense," Harper said as she reached for a drying towel. "We'll take care of it. Besides, Hardy just pulled up. I'm sure he'd love to catch up with you."

I smiled my thanks. She was right. We'd both been way busier than usual with cases and wedding planning. Plus, Izzy was getting more involved in extracurriculars, putting our downtime with each other at around twenty percent. She was staying the night at Mom's, giving us a little break to decompress.

The key sounded in the door, and Hardy walked in, holding something behind his back. When he spotted me, he smiled, and my heart skipped a beat.

"Aww," Fletcher cooed.

Harper snorted and shushed her.

Hardy nodded to my friends and walked into the living room, revealing a small bouquet and a cream-colored envelope. I sat on the couch and patted the seat beside me.

He handed everything over, sat beside me, and pulled me close. "How about we stop worrying about the wedding for a while and go on a trip?"

"Yes!" Fletcher shouted from the kitchen. "She says yes!"

Harper and Fletcher started bickering. I started laughing, and Hardy shook his head in bemusement. "Open the envelope," he said.

I gave him a curious glance, but broke the seal and pulled out an invitation card. My brain struggled to catch up with what my eyes were seeing, but once it did, my hands went clammy.

"Oh, my goodness," I squealed. "Is this for real?"

Hardy's eyes sparkled. "It is. Daniel pulled some strings for me." He rolled his eyes. "He will be attending as a guest, but I think the mansion is large enough to avoid him."

I laughed. Hardy and Daniel were a little like oil and water, but they held a mutual respect for each other. I flipped the card over to see the reservation confirmation and a small pile of tickets clipped together.

"Dinner and drinks," Hardy said. "Some are complimentary. The rest we have to pay for."

"Steinhoffer Mansion," I murmured. "I've always wanted to go there."

Hardy pressed a kiss to my hair. "I know. There's a rare manuscript exhibit arriving soon."

My breath caught. "And we have tickets?"

Hardy grinned. "And we have tickets."

I squealed and launched myself at him, pressing my lips against his.

I heard a few whispers from the kitchen and the soft sound of the front door shutting.

"Are you sure we can take the time off?" I stared down at the invitation, emotion welling inside me at Hardy's thoughtfulness.

"Who better to leave in charge of the shops than Harper and a retired FBI agent?" He chuckled. "Maybe leaving those two alone might shake some sense into them."

I glanced at him in surprise. "You feel it, too?"

Hardy rolled his eyes. "Those two could set the couch on fire if they sat down on it at the same time."

I snorted. "True."

Hardy slipped off his shoes and slid back onto the couch, tugging me with him until I was nestled in the crook of his arm.

"And Izzy?" I asked.

"Your mom and Gran have happily offered to spoil Izzy to pieces," he said in a droll tone.

"She'll never be the same."

"Probably not," he agreed.

"When do we leave?"

"Two days."

"I can't wait," I murmured.

Hardy wrapped his arms around me. "Neither can I."

THREE

I gawked at the mansion from the car window. Despite seeing the place dozens of times online and in magazines, there was no way to fully realize the scope until it loomed before me. Gray stone several stories high blocked out the weak midday sun. An attendant waved our vehicle in, and we followed behind three other cars into the main circular driveway.

Steinhoffer Mansion had been in the same family for several hundred years and now belonged to Maxwell Steinhoffer, an author of popular literary fiction. I found his work a little *too* literary for my tastes. Though I loved some of it, I leaned more toward genre fiction and adventure, but didn't mind a dash of romance here and there.

Maxwell Steinhoffer wrote sweeping family dynasties where not much happened except character growth and unrequited love. To each his own, I always said. However, he was wildly popular at my store, so I ensured I kept several of his works in stock. I was more interested in seeing the rare manuscript display, though I wouldn't sneeze at the chance to meet the author whose mansion I'd be staying at for a few days.

Hardy parked next to a massive stone water fountain, turned off for the season. Fresh snow glittered on the ground, undisturbed on most of the grounds. The day held a quiet, peaceful tone, and when Hardy turned the engine off, we sat in the car for a moment staring at the splendor before us.

"I feel like a bumpkin about to meet the queen," Hardy confessed, breaking the silence.

"Me too. I guess we could have a mansion if we really wanted one." Even a four-bedroom house was pushing it for me. I always believed love grew best in smaller spaces.

Hardy glanced at me curiously. "Do you want a mansion?"

"Not even a little bit."

His teeth flashed in a smile. "Me neither. Ready?"

"Yes, let us powder our noses before we meet the queen," I said, affecting a posh English accent.

Hardy and I got out of the car. "You look beautiful as always, princess," he drawled, holding his hand out for me.

We walked up to the front steps, where a man in a spiffy tuxedo awaited us. He greeted us with a nod and waited for the other people to gather around.

"Where's Daniel?" I whispered.

"I'm assuming he'll arrive by a flying golden carriage in the middle of the night," Hardy whispered back.

I snorted and squeezed his hand. "Jealousy is a terrible look on you," I teased.

He leaned close and whispered in my ear. "I'll show you exactly how jealous I am tonight."

My cheeks burned just as the tuxedo guy meaningfully cleared his throat. Hardy straightened with a grin.

I'd missed half of what the guy said, but it didn't seem to matter. The massive wooden double doors opened with an ominous creak, and we were ushered inside with little fanfare.

I gasped the second I stepped into the stunning corridor. Stained glass windows high above me let in sparkling, crystalline light that played over everyone's skin in a startling array of colors. A smile broke over my face as I held my arm out in front of me. Blues, reds, purples, and greens swirled over my forearm.

"Beautiful," I murmured.

"So, no mansion, but these windows are a yes?"

I nodded. "Definite yes, though I'd want something botanical instead of religious themed."

I wasn't sure what scene played above me, but there were angels and swords and some kind of heavenly battle. It was beautiful, but not something I'd want to look at every day. There was enough strife in the world without being reminded of it all the time.

Two other couples wandered behind us, gawking just as much as I had. The first couple was older than Hardy and me. If I had to guess, the woman was somewhere in her early fifties, and the man was maybe pushing sixty. She was short, blonde, and dressed in that cool, elegant way of the upper crust. The man was tall, with slightly hunched shoulders and a curious expression.

The other couple was around our age, maybe in their early twenties to late thirties. The woman was taller than me, thin and pale, but her eyes were friendly, and there were faint laugh lines around the edges of her mouth. This was a woman who smiled a lot. She wore a pair of straight-legged corduroy pants, a boat neck shirt, and a long tan cardigan with minimal jewelry and makeup.

The man I assumed was her partner was about the same height, leanly built and tan. He had light brown eyes and sandy-colored hair. He was dressed more corporate than she was—charcoal slacks, button-down shirt, shiny leather shoes, and a sweater I suspected might be cashmere.

Hardy and I were somewhere in the middle. I wore fleece-lined dark wash pants, knee-high boots, and a long, green sweater. Since the weather was so cold, I'd left my hair down, allowing it to fall over a deep purple scarf I'd carefully wound around my neck. Hardy was dressed in dark wash jeans, a grey pullover sweater, and a pair of well-worn brown loafers. My jewelry was a mishmash of pieces I'd picked up over the years from art fairs and sentimental pieces given to me by friends and family, topped off with the sparkling diamond on my left hand.

"I'll show you to your rooms," the man said. "You'll be staying on the third floor." He stopped and gestured to the left. "You've each received a packet detailing the schedule over the next few days. We won't make any exceptions if you're late for the events, nor will we delay any of the meals. The fourth floor is strictly off limits. Any locked doors are secured for a reason. The kitchens are closed and locked after 11 p.m. If you're caught in any unauthorized areas, you'll be promptly escorted from the grounds." A thin smile appeared on his lips. "If you read the fine print on your contract, you will notice a no questions asked, no refunds policy."

No one said a word, though the upper-crust woman huffed under her breath. I ducked my head to hide a smile and followed where the man gestured.

A few minutes later, a nameless bellhop dropped our luggage off and made himself scarce, leaving Hardy and me alone in a massive room with a glorious balcony overlooking the back of the grounds.

I held the schedule in my hand and read off the evening's festivities. "Cocktails at six p.m. Dinner at seven. Reading to follow right after dinner."

"A reading?" Hardy shrugged off his jacket and hung it on the hook by the door. "By whom?"

"Maxwell." I peered closer at the fine print. "It's from his upcoming work, *The Swallow and the Stork.*"

Hardy snorted. "That's a terrible name. What's it about?"

"I'm not sure," I admitted. "But I won't pass on the opportunity to hear him speak."

"You have a weakness for authors."

I looked up from the schedule and smiled at him. "Not

that much of a weakness. Otherwise, Daniel might have lured me here instead of you."

Hardy laughed as he took a seat on the expensive couch. "True." He laced his hands behind his head and put his feet on the coffee table. "I *am* way better than an author." He winked and patted the place next to him.

Once I settled next to him, he let out a long sigh. "How about we skip cocktail hour?"

I smile against his chest. "Sold."

FOUR

Dinner was a four-course culinary delight filled with classical music streaming through high-quality speakers and awkward conversation in between courses. I wasn't here for them anyway, so the lack of sparkling conversation didn't bother me. Hardy put his hand on my knee and squeezed.

"Want to sleep in tomorrow?" he murmured in my ear.

I grinned. "Sounds heavenly."

Dinner finished with little fanfare. Once the servers refilled our drinks, we filed from the room and followed our illustrious stoic leader down the hall into a small drawing room with a crackling fireplace.

A middle-aged man sat in a large leather chair to the right side. He held a leather-bound journal in one hand and a smoldering pipe in the other. He smiled politely and gestured us all in.

Maxwell was more handsome than I expected. He had

wavy brown hair and jade-green eyes reflecting a piercing intellect, straight white teeth, and a relaxed manner. He wore a pair of brown pants and a cream-colored pullover sweater.

When we were all settled in, Maxwell began to speak. And as he did, I realized why an entire generation of readers hung on his every word. This new book sounded fascinating, and I made a mental note to order extra copies for the shop.

The doors opened halfway through the session, revealing a familiar face. Daniel Jensen waved, quietly crept in, and settled into a chair next to Hardy.

Maxwell nodded at Daniel and kept reading.

When he finished, everyone broke into wild applause, Daniel included. Maxwell stood and offered to stay for a little while and chat. Hardy and I waited for everyone to surround him before sneaking another drink off a cart to wait our turn.

Daniel stayed back with us and brought me into a warm hug. "Dakota, Hardy. Always nice to see one of you."

Hardy chuckled. "Daniel. Always a pleasure."

The two men shook hands.

"I'm glad you two decided to come out. It's not every day Max allows guests in his compound."

"You know each other?" I asked. The publishing world was small, so it wasn't out of the realm of possibility for authors to know each other.

"We were college roommates."

I gawked. "Seriously? And you never told me?"

Daniel's expression turned amused. "Have we ever talked about college?"

I frowned. "Some things you should always tell your friends."

He offered a tiny bow. "Then I shall endeavor to tell you everything about myself in the future. Even the tiniest detail."

I snorted. "No need for sarcasm."

Daniel grinned. "Would you like to meet him?"

Hardy put a hand over his heart. "Another author to steal my love away," he said dramatically.

I laughed and smacked him on his shoulder. "Hardly. It's part of the job."

Daniel winked and offered me his elbow. "Come. I'll shoo everyone away and give you a personal introduction."

"And he's an enabler," Hardy sighed.

He grinned at my fiancé and tugged me in Max's direction.

The author nodded and made his excuses, coming over to stand close to the fireplace beside us. "Max, this is my dear friend, Dakota Adair. She owns a lovely little bookshop in Silverwood Hollow."

Max's eyes lit up. "That's a wonderful place. I've been through there a couple of times, but I only remember one bookshop, and I don't recall ever seeing you there."

"I bought it a few years ago," I said as I stuck my hand out to shake his.

"Ah. New ownership." We shook hands, and I was

surprised to feel how calloused his palms were. This was a man who worked with his hands away from a laptop. "You had a great selection in there."

My smile slipped. "Still do," I said, "though the genre fiction section is much larger than it used to be."

Max's lips quirked in amusement. "I see. You read those gauche vampire novels?"

I'd spoken to this guy for mere seconds, and I already didn't like him. "No, I prefer murder. Though I'm not opposed to vampire fiction. Sometimes paranormal creatures are more tolerable than humans."

Daniel squeezed my elbow in warning.

Max chuckled. "Beautiful and witty. It's been a while since I've had a guest like you." He waved his hand toward the back. "Would you like to see my private library?"

Those eight little words could seduce legions of book lovers all over the world. I glanced at Hardy, who was watching me with lifted eyebrows. He jerked his head toward the library.

"Go ahead," he mouthed.

"I would love to," I said, curling my hand around Daniel's elbow.

Max's eyes sparkled. "Allow me to say my goodbyes, then."

A few minutes later, I stood in a stunning library with polished two-story high shelves filled with thousands of books. The room smelled of lemon polish and pipe smoke, an odd but tantalizing combination.

"This is amazing," I breathed.

"Please." Max waved his hand around the room. "Feel free to explore. I'll catch up with Daniel."

I blinked. "Are you sure?"

"Quite. It's not often I find a true book lover. Someone can love an author or a genre, but rarely does someone devote their entire life to books. They are meant to be shared, no?"

I gave him a grateful smile and headed off to see what I could find. Daniel gave me a long look. I wiggled my brows at him before turning away.

Max's library wasn't contained to a single room. After exploring for a while, I looked over and noticed the two men deep in conversation, their heads together while they studied a massive leather tome.

Shrugging, I opened the door looming in front of me. It swung open without a sound, bringing with it the smell of old books and leather. Stepping inside, the air felt cooler, crisper. I wondered if he had a dehumidifier inside. If he did, it meant the books inside this room held more value than the ones in the main area.

I rubbed my hands together in glee. Max's collection was the largest private library I'd ever seen, surpassing even Daniel's. A smile tugged at my lips. I couldn't wait to rub this in his face. As much as I liked Daniel, he sometimes acted a little too big for his britches. This might take him down a couple of pegs.

After exploring for a while, making mental notes to ask about a few of the books in his collection, I plucked an interesting selection from the shelf and settled into one of the several seating areas to read for a while.

The noise of hushed conversation eventually pulled me from my reverie. I shut the book and strained to listen. The additional part of the library was smaller than the first area Max showed me, but it was still large enough to accommodate several people without running into one another.

I heard a male and female voice. Neither sounded familiar.

"Are you kidding?" the female hissed. "I asked you about this weeks ago! You said you were going to take care of it."

"I'm trying. Things like that don't happen overnight."

"I came here for you," the woman whined. "And you brought her here."

I cringed. Should I announce myself? Try to sneak out?

The man sighed. "I had to. She got too curious."

I rolled my eyes and carefully set my book down before easing from my chair.

"Get rid of her," she murmured.

"I can't tell her to go home," he said. "She's my wife."

"Not for long." The woman's tone turned seductive. "We have to take care of this soon. I can't keep waiting for you."

"No." His voice went rough. "This will happen on my timeline. Not yours."

The woman gasped. "I gave you everything you

wanted! How dare you? It's now or never. If you don't want this, someone else will. Think of all you'll lose."

"I'll lose nothing," the man growled. A bumping sound echoed through the room. My brows furrowed. I took a hesitant step in their direction but stopped. This was none of my business. If I got involved, it would ruin our vacation. Hardy would be upset, and so would our host. Shaking my head, I turned toward the door and had made it almost to the end of the room when I heard another bump, louder this time, and the sound of books crashing to the floor.

I spun toward the sound. A female scream sounded before being abruptly cut off.

"I said no," the male voice growled. "Don't get involved."

There was a feminine gasp and some whispering I couldn't make out.

I hurried through the room, rounding the corner, cursing at how long it was taking me to navigate all the obstacles, only to see a male looming over a prone woman lying on the ground.

"Hey!" I shouted.

The man's shoulders jerked. He didn't turn to look at me. Instead, he hurtled the opposite way.

My instincts urged me to go after him, but the woman was hurt. Blood pooled under her body, and I dropped to my knees, shrugging off my cardigan to press to her stomach. "Daniel!" I shouted. "Daniel!"

A few seconds later, the door boomed open. "Dakota? Are you okay?"

"Back here! Hurry! Do you have your cell?"

A few seconds later, Daniel rounded the same corner and cursed as soon as he saw me.

"Call 911," I urged.

Daniel fumbled with his phone. I reached to check the woman's pulse. It was thready and weak, and she was too pale. Red hair spilled around her shoulders, and her eyes were wide with shock. She was young and pretty, modestly dressed in slacks and a blouse. Not a typical outfit for an affair partner, if that's what she was.

"Stay with me," I whispered, brushing my hand over her face.

Max's face appeared around the corner, his brow furrowed. "Dakota? What on earth?" His face turned ashen when he saw the woman on the ground.

Daniel spoke to the 911 operator. I pressed my hand against the woman's abdomen and kept telling her she would be okay, even though I knew it would be a lie.

"An ambulance is on its way," Daniel said, tucking his phone back into his pocket.

Max came closer. "What—who is that?"

I shook my head. "No idea. I was hoping you'd know."

"No. My assistant said two more couples checked in late, but neither made the reading."

A thought occurred to me. "Did someone come in on their own? A single occupancy?"

Max pressed his lips together. "I wouldn't know. You'd have to talk to Tess."

"Tess?" I questioned.

"My assistant. She handles all the event planning and booking. She'd know everyone scheduled to attend."

Daniel crouched down beside me. "Want me to take over?"

I shook my head. "No. I don't want to let up on the pressure. Can you call Hardy?"

"Of course." Daniel took his phone out and made the call.

It was less than a minute before Hardy found me. His eyes took in the scene, then me, and his face softened in sympathy.

Daniel rose and patted me on the shoulder. Hardy took his place, reaching over to press his fingers against the woman's pulse. His lips turned down.

"Keep pressure on the wound," he said. Hardy moved to the other side and began to perform CPR.

Not long after, paramedics entered. Hardy gently eased me away from the woman. "Let's get cleaned up," he said in a low voice.

"I should stay," I said, shrugging away from him.

"Dakota. Let them do their work."

Tears sprang to my eyes as Hardy led me away. He flashed his consultant badge and murmured something to the head paramedic, who nodded, his eyes resting on me.

Max stepped up. "There's a back way."

I forgot to tell Hardy. "That's where he went." I

pointed to the area where the man ran away. "He killed her."

Hardy's posture tightened. His hand rested on his waistband, but there was no gun. "Stay behind me."

Max looked between us.

"I'll lead," Hardy said. "Tell me where we need to go."

I followed behind my fiancé, shaking my head at the awful turn the evening had taken.

I'd potentially witnessed a murder and been too late to stop it.

FIVE

Sometime later, I was physically cleaned up but still an emotional mess. After a quick phone call, Quinn had contacted the local police and convinced them to give us a little time before they grilled me about what happened.

Hardy had gently asked me a dozen questions before he felt ready for me to go back in and face the authorities. Whoever the man was who killed that woman was long gone. Or at least long gone from the crime scene.

He had to be a guest staying here for the event, but I couldn't have picked him out in a lineup. Cursing my introverted tendencies, I let Hardy escort me back toward Max's study.

Neither of us had spoken to any of the other guests, so I might be unable to identify who had been speaking even if I heard it again. They'd kept their voices low, almost in hushed whispers.

"Just stick to the facts. Nothing else," Hardy urged as he opened the door.

More than likely the killer was still here. Leaving so quickly would only rouse suspicion, but the thought of going to dinner each night with a killer made my blood run cold. Inside, Max and two other police officers waited for us. He sat in his leather chair, his face still pale and eyes wide with shock. The officers sat on the maroon couch, leaving Hardy and me to take the loveseat.

I folded my hands in my lap and waited. This was familiar ground, even though I never expected to be here again. I guess my life had come full circle. It was funny in a way. Being a suspect in a murder was how I met Hardy, and now he was sitting beside me, holding my hand to help me through it. Life could be strange, that's for sure.

The female officer's name tag read Rooney. She was small and pretty and stared at me with a blank expression. Typical cop face. I wouldn't get any help from her. The man next to her was largely built and had a wide, friendly face with crow's feet at the edge of his eyes. He smiled at me and pulled his notebook out. "Miss Adair?"

I nodded.

"I'm Kevin Waters. This is my partner, Ruby. Thanks for coming to speak with us."

I smiled tightly. Not like I had a choice. Hardy tightened his grip on my hand.

"I understand you were a witness to this crime?"

"Sort of," I began. Recounting the story was harder

than I expected, and by the end, my entire body was trembling. Hardy scooted a little closer.

"Is there anything else you can tell us?" Kevin asked. Ruby hadn't said a word the entire time, only watched me closely. I felt like I was sitting in front of a lie detector machine.

"I don't think so. He never turned around, so I didn't get a look at his face. The lighting isn't great in here, but he appeared to be Caucasian and maybe around six feet. I only saw him for a few seconds before he took off."

The officer closed his notebook. "Thank you, Miss Adair." He pulled a card from his front pocket and handed it to me. "Call me if you think of anything else."

I tucked the card away. "Are we free to leave?"

Hardy stiffened beside me.

Ruby and Kevin exchanged a look. "I'm afraid not, ma'am. We'd like everyone to stick around for the next few days. We're leaving a few officers on the premises to prevent anyone from leaving the grounds."

My eyebrows lifted.

"I'm sorry?" Hardy leaned forward. "You can't make us stay here for longer than necessary."

Kevin's eyes hardened. "I'm afraid we can, Mr. Cavanaugh. The governor has a vested interest in seeing this crime solved."

Max looked down at his feet and said nothing.

"The governor?" I asked faintly.

Hardy swore. I pulled out my phone and texted Daniel.

BOOK CLUB BAIT & SWITCH 33

Ruby, the quiet officer, grinned maliciously. "He's inquired about purchasing this property from Mr. Steinhoffer. Having an unsolved murder on the premises is not ideal."

I let out a heavy sigh. Daniel stepped into the room a few moments later, eyeing Max with disappointment.

Kevin glanced at him and frowned. "I'm sorry. This area is off limits for the next little while."

"Miss Adair asked me to come in," Daniel said, breezing past the other officers to come and stand behind me. "Apparently, we've gone from vacay to locked in an Agatha Christie novel, have we?" His words were for Max, who blushed crimson and refused to look at him. "Even with all this wealth, you couldn't help but want more."

The disapproval in Daniel's voice was palpable. Hardy watched him, and something flashed in my fiancé's eyes. Respect, perhaps. Either way, Max stood abruptly. "I don't have to listen to this," he snapped before storming out of the room.

No one said anything for a long moment.

"Can they really keep us here?" I asked.

Hardy sighed. "For a little while, yes. But throwing the governor in the mix complicates things." He shook his head and addressed the officers. "How long are we expected to stay?"

Kevin shrugged. "Depends on how fast we can find who did this."

Hardy and I exchanged a look. Daniel chuckled under his breath and straightened. "I expect you'll find that with

Dakota and Hardy in the mix, solving your case will happen much faster than anticipated."

The officer's brow furrowed, but before he could say anything, Daniel strode out the door.

"Troublemaker," Hardy muttered.

Ruby leaned forward, eyes glittering. "Is there going to be any trouble from you two?"

Hardy put a warning hand on my thigh. He smiled, but it didn't reach his eyes. "Not from us."

"Good." Ruby rose and headed toward the door.

Kevin watched her go and returned his attention to us as he shut his notebook. "You're former law enforcement."

Hardy nodded.

"And your...wife?" He didn't seem angry about it, more curious than anything.

"Almost wife," Hardy said with a smile. "She's a private investigator."

"And I own a bookshop," I interjected, feeling the need to tell him even though it wasn't relevant.

Amusement flashed over his face. "A bookshop owning private investigator? Sounds like a novel."

Boy did it. One day I might try to write about all these adventures.

"I've lived an interesting life."

Kevin tucked his pen away and opened his mouth to say something before shutting it and shaking his head.

"You can tell us not to look into things, but I'm afraid the words will fall on deaf ears." Hardy's smile was rueful.

I elbowed him.

The officer stood and handed Hardy a business card. "I was thinking about the opposite, actually," he admitted. "It's hard to go poking around when the focus is on someone like Max." He grimaced. "Now that the governor has a vested interest, it will make the case twice as difficult." He walked to the door and looked back. "If there were already people on the inside, it would make looking into things much easier. And," he said as he tapped on the door frame, "the local police department would be extremely grateful for any assistance."

Hardy saluted him with the extra business card. "Happy to help."

We waited until the room was empty before speaking again.

"I shouldn't be surprised that our first vacation turned into a locked-room murder mystery." Hardy dragged a hand through his hair and sighed.

I grimaced. "Sorry."

He slid a glance my way and smirked. "It's not your fault, though I wonder if you have some kind of karmic load you still haven't repaid."

Hardy laughed at my outraged look and pulled me closer. "I'm kidding. You've helped a lot of people. Don't start second-guessing yourself now."

I sighed and stood. "Since we're unofficially on the case, should we look around?"

Hardy groaned. "Quickly, then we're going to bed. It's been a long day."

That was the understatement of the year.

SIX

The room yielded little to assist us. Tomorrow would be better. A group breakfast was scheduled for the morning, and everyone was encouraged to attend because the details for the first day of the event would be given out.

Hardy and I went to bed around midnight. When the alarm went off the next morning, both of us let out loud groans.

I cracked an eye open and saw Hardy frowning. "Do we have to go?"

His lips tipped in a smile. "Unfortunately. If we want to get out of here, we have to attend every event on the schedule."

"Yay," I said sarcastically.

He rolled over and pulled me close. "I'm going to call Quinn and see if he can bring Poppy by."

I blinked. "This doesn't seem like a place that would allow pets."

"Don't care," Hardy murmured against my hair. "Daniel already said to do it."

I stilled. "Daniel?"

I felt his smile. "Yep. Regardless of what you might think, I actually like the guy."

Maybe I didn't understand male friendships well enough. When women became friends, we lifted each other up. When men became friends, they did a lot of insulting. Sighing, I shook my head and let it go. "Daniel said it's okay to get Poppy?" I had to admit, I'd rarely been away from her for long. It'd be nice to have her around.

"He knows Max from way back. Now that we're here to help, Max has softened his stance on what he will and won't allow."

"How gracious of him," I muttered.

"I figure Quinn can come in and we can see how Poppy will adjust. I'll call Kevin this morning and have Quinn cleared."

Reluctantly, I rolled out of the warmth of Hardy's arms. "Shouldn't be too hard. He's former law enforcement."

Hardy pulled the covers up to his chin. "If he can stay longer and assist, even better."

"I wonder if there are any more rooms available." As soon as I said it, I laughed. This place was enormous. We weren't just in a mansion. This place looked like a compound.

"We'll find somewhere for him to stay."

"Not in here, please." I liked Quinn, but we fought like siblings.

Hardy yanked my hand, tilting me off balance, before he struck like a snake, wrapping an arm around my waist and pulling me back under the covers. I shrieked a laugh and half-heartedly tried to pull away.

"Five more minutes," he pleaded.

"How can I say no to that?"

Hardy cackled triumphantly and pulled the covers over our heads.

What a way to start the day.

WE ROLLED into the group breakfast five minutes early, which from the amount of people already inside, meant we were late. I elbowed Hardy. "Told you so."

He grinned. "Worth it."

I laughed in spite of myself. "How do you want to do this? I take the girls, you take the guys?"

He tilted his head and studied the room. A massive rectangular table with an embroidered tablecloth sat in the middle, surrounded by a dozen mahogany chairs. Behind the table loomed a massive window with the curtains opened, allowing the morning sunlight to stream inside. The light cast a warm glow on the silver tableware, making the entire scene look like something from Normal Rockwell.

Hints of herbs teased my nose, and my stomach growled.

"How about we sit down and eat first before we grill everyone?" Without waiting for an answer, Hardy led me inside and settled us toward the middle of the table, where two seats were left open.

There were six couples milling around, along with a few harried waitstaff carrying large silver coffee carafes and clean mugs. I nodded to the few who glanced our way before returning my attention to the mug above my plate. Before seating himself, he took both mugs.

"Get comfortable. I'll be back."

"Bless you," I murmured. Coffee was way more important than food this early in the morning.

I shrugged my cardigan off and lay it across the back of my chair before I sat down. A bell chimed three times, signaling the beginning of the meal. Hardy returned and set a steaming mug before me and settled in beside me.

"Good morning," a voice said.

I craned my neck around to see Max walking into the room. He wore a warm smile that didn't reach his eyes. This morning, he looked like the epitome of an eccentric author. He wore a pair of brown corduroy pants, a cream-colored sweater, and brown loafers. A scarf was tied loosely around his neck.

His cologne trickled into the room—a spicy, woodsy combination. Pleasant, but I refused to like it simply because I didn't like Max very much.

"Stop frowning," Hardy whispered in my ear.

I smoothed my face.

He put his hand on my knee. "I know you don't like

him, but we can't let that get in the way of what we're trying to do."

"Is he married?" I whispered back.

The couple across the table sent us a dirty look. I smiled politely.

"No idea."

Daniel crept in late and took the seat beside me. Max kept droning on, pausing for a moment to give Daniel a baleful look. He ignored it and reached for my coffee cup, taking a giant swig before I could stop him.

I reached over and pinched him on the side, but he wore a thick sweater, and I couldn't get much skin. He wiggled his eyebrows at me and gave my mug back. When Max finally stopped talking and settled himself at the head of the table, conversation struck back up, and Daniel leaned over.

"So," he drawled, "who's first on the list?"

My eyebrows lifted. "List?"

"Mmm hmm. Who are you interrogating first?"

I snorted. "I don't interrogate. I simply ask questions."

He nodded sagely. "Sure you do. Which one then?" His gaze swept back and forth. "Hmm. I don't think everyone is here yet."

"How many extra couples arrived yesterday?"

He lifted a shoulder. "No idea. Two was the last number I heard."

I thought about what Max had said yesterday. "Do you know who Tess is?"

"Pretty girl at the front desk. Young and blonde."

I eyed him. "Did you ask her any questions?"

Daniel lay a hand over his heart. "I am merely a starving artist, Dakota, not a trained and licensed private investigator."

I rolled my eyes. "Let me guess. You got her number?"

Daniel grinned. "My true heart's desire callously accepted another man's proposal. Am I to be a poor, lonely wretch forever?"

"No," I said dryly. "Just a drama queen."

Hardy chuckled.

The bell rang again. Doors I didn't realize were there opened seamlessly, revealing a sea of waitstaff holding trays and pitchers.

Within minutes, our plates were piled high, and our drinks refilled. Conversation died while everyone ate, and I took the time to study everyone. The first two I'd seen yesterday sat a few chairs down, the older couple dressed meticulously again this early. She had a small poached egg and a slice of toast on her plate. He had an egg white scramble and a lonely slice of bacon.

The younger couple ate a little heartier, though the woman's plate was full of potatoes and fruit. I wondered if she was a vegetarian. Our eyes met, and she smiled, her brown eyes friendly but cool.

Daniel leaned in. "Anyone hitting your radar?"

I rolled my eyes. "It's barely seven in the morning. Nothing is hitting my radar until coffee warms all my gears up."

Hardy leaned over. "Do you find it odd that no one is talking about the murder?"

I frowned. That was weird. "Is it possible they don't know?" I whispered.

"I wouldn't think so, but it seems likely." Hardy shook his head. "Rich people."

Daniel's eyes swept the table. "The woman wearing pearls seems like she hates her husband," he whispered.

I choked on my coffee.

That particular woman sat close to Max on the opposite end of the table. Her hair was styled in a perfect chignon, and her makeup was elegant and understated. She wore a crisp white blouse with chunky gold jewelry. I admired her ability to keep her blouse unstained in a buffet environment. There was a reason I wore a lot of dark colors.

Beside her sat a well-dressed man who looked like he never smiled a day in his life. His eyes were focused on cutting his sausage, and he stayed silent.

Max cleared his throat. "I hope the breakfast was worthy of such esteemed company," he began.

A few people clapped politely. Max's smile didn't reach his eyes. "I thought this might be a good time to introduce ourselves."

I groaned inwardly. He'd just announced the introvert's worst nightmare—talking about oneself in a public environment—but it would allow us to put names to faces and see if anyone was acting weird.

Hardy sat a little straighter and paid attention. The

couple on the opposite side of the one I'd just noticed spoke up. They were much younger than all of us, maybe early to mid-twenties. The female was wide-eyed and soft-spoken.

Her fiancé did most of the talking. They were from Kentucky and about to marry in the spring. Although they seemed enamored with each other, I knew better than to put stock into anything on the surface. She said her name was Wendy, and his was Brian. No children unless you counted their Chihuahua, Chichi. Which I didn't.

The woman in the chignon with the sour husband had flown all the way from California. She introduced herself as Chelsea and claimed to own a rare bookshop in wine country and was a big fan of Max if the way she preened under her attention was any indication. The man beside her grunted, said he was an art restorer, and his name was Cliff. They looked about as complementary together as peanut butter and mustard.

And so it went. The older couple we'd first seen introduced themselves as Mary and Heath James. They owned a winery in Michigan. The younger couple was named Kristy and David Brauer. Both of them did something in tech.

Another couple said they came from a couple of hours away. They owned a small business they refused to disclose. Hailey and Richard were their names. I couldn't get much of a read on either one. Both were closed-lipped and unfriendly.

The next couple were much friendlier. The wife,

Samantha, owned a bakery specializing in wedding cakes, which perked me right up, and the husband, Nick, retired young after some good investments.

"Why didn't you retire, too?" Daniel asked.

Samantha smiled. "Sometimes a job isn't a job. It's a calling."

I liked her right away.

Max interrupted. "Our last two couples came in late last night, so they may seem unfamiliar, but they are both personal friends of mine." He smiled and gestured for them to take the floor.

The first woman was tall and willowy and had soft red hair. She sat next to a handsome blond man. "I'm Sarah, and this is my husband, Mike. He's an author and I'm an editor for a literary press."

Mike, an odd-looking little man, gave a weird little salute and smiled at us. He had a head of wild, curly hair and shifty eyes.

"A talented author," Max emphasized. "He may be bigger than me one day."

Everyone chuckled politely, and I suppressed the urge to roll my eyes.

Mike lay a hand over his heart. "One can dream," he demurred.

But Max's smile felt off. I looked between him and Mike and made a mental note to do some digging there.

The last couple was also our age. Temperance worked as a museum curator, and her husband, Luke, was an archaeologist.

"Temperance is a wealth of information, and I've leaned on her multiple times for book research."

She tilted her head. "Always happy to help."

Luke said nothing, only watched Max with a slight curl to his lip.

Interesting. I nudged Hardy, but he was already watching them.

"Wonderful." Max clapped his hands. "I have work to do so I'll retire to my chambers. However, I will return at six p.m. to unveil the details of the traveling manuscript. Until then, you are free to explore the grounds at your leisure, keeping in mind the rules set forth from yesterday." With a small smile, Max rose and gave us a little bow before exiting.

"He's insufferable," I muttered under my breath.

Daniel laughed. "You would be, too, if you had as many adoring fans as he does."

I slid him a wry look. "And you don't?"

His eyes glimmered with amusement. "I have my fair share, but this guy has legions. They fall all over him." Daniel rolled his eyes. "You should see how he struts around at his signings."

I poked him. "You sound jealous."

"Of course I'm jealous!" He batted his eyelashes at me. "Dakota, tell me, do you find him more handsome than me?"

Hardy leaned forward and peered at him. "Do not answer that."

Daniel barked a laugh. "Even Hardy thinks I'm more

handsome than him. I suppose that will help me sleep tonight."

I rolled my eyes and stood up. "Come on, you two. Let's see if we can get anything out of these people."

By then everyone was shuffling into makeshift groups, testing the waters to see if they'd be a good match to spend the next few days with. It felt like some sort of odd mating ritual, but I was about to stomp all over their ritual and insert myself awkwardly into their groups in order to get the information we needed.

Curious that no one knew about the murder, though. Police were crawling all over the place last night, along with EMTs and medical professionals, even the coroner. How in the world had they managed to bypass everyone inside the mansion and take the body out without anyone noticing?

Hardy stood a few feet away, introducing himself to the museum lady and her husband. I made a beeline for the coffee carafe. Mary stood there, her cool blonde hair swept away from her face.

"Good morning." I smiled as I stepped up beside her.

She glanced my way. "Morning." Her voice was clipped and cultured. She wore a pair of slim-fit ankle pants with suede loafers and an oversized white button-down tunic. Gold jewelry glinted at her throat and wrists. Mary was the picture of cool elegance.

"The breakfast was wonderful. I wonder if Max eats like that all the time."

"I suppose he does," Mary said. She stepped away to doctor her coffee.

"I'm more of a grab a muffin and rush to work kind of girl."

"Mmm."

I need to try another tack. "How is it owning a winery? Since it's Michigan, I assume it's seasonal."

Her eyes brightened. "Yes. We have quite rowdy winters." Mary moved over so I could fix my coffee. "Are you a wine drinker?"

Oh, how I disliked small talk. "I've never met a Pinot Noir I dislike."

Mary laughed, the first genuine thing I'd heard from her. "I'll have to steal that one."

I wanted to scream, *Did you murder someone?* Instead, I laughed with her and turned to watch the other couples milling about. "What brought you to this retreat?"

Mary shrugged. "It was mostly Heath's idea. He's a big fan of Max and has a little history with him. I guess he wanted to catch up." Her lips pursed. "And knowing my husband, he wanted to test the waters to see if Max might be willing to sponsor one of our wines."

Interesting. "Did you bring any bottles with you?"

Mary chuckled. "An entire case of our best." She eyed me for a moment. "How about you and your fiancé come up to our quarters this evening to share a bottle? We've already invited another couple, so six people is perfect! We'll have to open two then."

I glanced at Hardy. "We'd love to. What time?"

We chatted a bit more and set a time to meet before Mary excused herself and wandered over to Heath. One down. Several more to go.

I noticed the tech couple over by themselves speaking quietly. When they noticed me looking, I raised my hand in a wave and made my way over.

"I'm Dakota," I said with a polite smile.

"The bookstore owner, right?" Kristy said.

During our intro, we conveniently left out the fact that we were private investigators. No need to spook the masses. Yet.

"That's right. We don't specialize in one genre, but I do have a weakness for crime thrillers, so I carry more of those than normal."

Kristy laughed. "As much as I love Max's work, I'm afraid it doesn't cross over into other literary fiction. Crime thrillers are one of my favorites, but I also love the occasional escapist fantasy."

"Oh? Which books?"

She rattled off Robin Hobb and a few others, then mentioned a couple I hadn't heard of, so I got my cell out and typed those into my notes section.

David, her husband, nodded occasionally but didn't jump into the conversation. "What about you?" I asked. "Are you a closet genre fiction lover?"

He shook his head. "I read mostly non-fiction but occasionally listen to Kristy prattle on about her newest fantasy read."

My smile froze for an instant. How...mean. "Well," I

said, "my poor fiancé has been held hostage numerous times when I've found a particular book I love, but that's the price of marriage, isn't it? Supporting the things your partner loves too?"

David's eyes tightened at the edges, and a brief but awkward silence followed before he let out a jovial laugh, breaking the tension. "I suppose that's a great way to put it! I've never seen the allure of a fantasy world when there are so many interesting things going on in the real world, but I suppose to each his own, right?"

Kristy's smile faded.

"That's what I love about it, actually. Fantasy offers an escape from the world's harshest realities. It's the perfect escape after a stressful day. Wouldn't you agree, Kristy?"

The woman glanced at me with wide eyes, a grateful smile crossing her lips before she nodded. "Yes, that's a wonderful way to put it. I favor strong female heroines who save themselves and conflicted villains. What about you?"

"Same," I sighed. "As I've grown older, I realize I identify more and more with the villain than the good guys."

We shared a laugh and chatted for a few minutes more before David pulled her away. I liked Kristy and didn't find out much about the murder, but I suspected David was less nice to Kristy at home than he was here, and that was saying something. While I spotted no telltale signs of physical abuse, Kristy flinched every time David gestured with his hands. Shoving my hands in my pockets, I watched his fingers tighten around Kristy's elbow as he pulled her away. Something was definitely off with those two.

Hardy came over and stood beside me. "Everything okay?" he murmured quietly.

A sigh escaped me. "A suspicion I'll tell you about later."

One of his eyebrows rose. "All right then." He glanced toward the door. "There's one more couple. Chelsea and Cliff."

"Dibs!" Those two owned the rare books store.

Hardy grinned. "Thought you might say that. Just make it over there before Daniel does. Want to take a tour of the grounds a little later?" He checked his watch. "Quinn should be here around lunchtime."

"Sounds great." I waved and headed over to the last couple. Chelsea and Cliff stood by the pastry table, each holding a bear claw. I couldn't eat another bite after breakfast, but I hadn't eaten like a bird either.

"Hello. I'm making the rounds introducing myself."

Chelsea nodded. "Dakota, correct?"

"Yes, and you're Chelsea and David?"

They both nodded. "Seems we're both bookstore owners. I don't specialize in rare books, but I have a few for sale."

Chelsea's face brightened. "Oh? Which one was your favorite?"

I thought about it. These two were obviously well off. They practically screamed money, so to get them to open up, I had to pull out the big guns. "I briefly held an original Audubon work."

Chelsea's eyes narrowed. "Wait. Is this the one that recently sold for millions?"

I wasn't surprised she'd heard about that. "It is."

"Interesting," she murmured. "There were very few details about that find in the articles I pulled up."

I smiled politely, feeling a squirm of unease in my stomach. "I'm sure the person it went to wanted to stay private. I held the books and plates briefly in my possession before a curator came to pick them up. As much as it pains me, I haven't seen them since. I can only assume they went to a very wealthy private collector."

"Mmm," she said, eyeing me in a way I didn't like.

"How about you? Has there been a book you didn't want to get rid of?"

She waved a hand. "Oh. Several. My favorite was an original Gutenberg Bible."

I almost swallowed my tongue. "Wow. First edition?"

She gave me a withering look. "Of course, darling. We rarely pick up books other than first editions."

It took a lot of effort to resist the urge to roll my eyes. "That must have been incredible to hold."

"It was. Holding history in your hands is an indescribable feeling. Right, Cliff?"

Cliff grunted once again.

"As an art restorer, you must have wonderful stories, too. Have you restored any paintings of note?"

He set his pastry down. "I helped with the restoration of Notre Dame."

I blinked. "Holy smokes," I breathed. "That's incredible."

He grunted again. "Real shame about that fire. I do what I can with the tools I have, and even then, sometimes it's not enough."

"It's an incredible piece of architecture. What did it feel like roaming through those halls?"

Cliff stared at me for a long moment, his pale blue eyes somber. "Like God Himself had touched me on the shoulder."

Silence fell between us. Tears pricked the back of my eyes, and I struggled to speak. Cliff wasn't sour at all, and guilt filled me at my misjudgment. Maybe he was deeper than all of us put together.

"Oh Cliff," Chelsea chided. "Always so intense."

His lips thinned, and he looked away.

"No," I breathed. "Art and history are things we should never take for granted. Imagine if art faded away. What would we be left with?" I gestured around the room. "None of this would exist."

Cliff grunted in agreement. "That's right. Art is in everything. Speaking, writing, our actions." He nodded at me. "I appreciate meeting someone who feels its impact as much as I do." With that Cliff wandered away. Chelsea clicked her tongue at his back. "I swear that man makes every conversation awkward."

"No," I murmured. "That was the best conversation I've had since I got here."

Chelsea looked taken aback. I smiled and said my goodbyes before wandering away. Again, I hadn't gotten any intel about the woman's death, but I'd met a very interesting man I hoped I got to talk to again.

I made a mental note to look Cliff up and see if he had an online work portfolio. He must be quite talented if he was tapped to work on Notre Dame.

Shaking my head, I went to find Hardy.

SEVEN

"Sounds like you have a crush on ol' Cliff," Hardy said with amusement after letting me sing the restorer's praise for the last fifteen minutes.

"It's the old soul," Daniel said. "It's her Achilles heel. Put a man in front of her who appreciates art as much as she does, and she's forever lost."

I snorted. "Hardly. You didn't impress me nearly as much as you thought you did."

Daniel laughed and lay a hand over his heart. "Ouch. How you wound me."

Hardy slung an arm over my shoulder. "Where should we start? The greenhouse? The gardens?"

"How about we walk the entire property?" Daniel suggested. "It's a beautiful day out and we have nothing better to do."

"Except find a murderer," I said dryly.

"What better way to do that than to explore?" Daniel

asked. "You never know when we might wander upon some lonely soul dying to tell us his employer's secrets."

I doubted it would be that easy. Hardy shrugged. "Up to you. We still have at least two hours before Quinn gets here, so it might not be a bad idea."

"Fine by me." We set out the back door and walked down a white stone path. Oak trees dotted our path, snow-tipped and majestic. Oaks weren't true evergreens, so they didn't lose their leaves until much later in winter. "Tell me what you found out. If anything," I added.

Daniel sighed. "I received two requests for free signed copies of my books and one invitation to after dinner drinks from a couple who looked far too interested in me for my comfort."

Hardy snorted. "Oh, to be famous."

"And rich," Daniel said with a smirk.

"Can it, you toddlers," I said fondly.

Daniel sighed dramatically. "What about you?" he said to Hardy. "Anything interesting?"

Hardy shrugged. "No one seems to know about the death. I have to admire Max's ability to hide information."

"His library had no windows," Daniel observed. "I never thought to check to see whether any of the windows faced toward the front door."

Hardy's brow furrowed. "That's a good catch. If no one could see out the window, and they didn't see anyone coming through the front door, maybe Max had them enter and exit through another area."

"He doesn't want the attention." Daniel shook his head. "Clever."

"Agreed, but it's going to make our job three times harder," I said.

Hardy shook his head. "Something isn't right here. Everyone should know by now because the police should have questioned them."

I slowed my steps and gawked up at him. "I can't believe I didn't think of that. Why in the world didn't that happen?"

"Money."

We looked back at Daniel who wore a thunderous expression. "Ten to one the entire police force is bought and paid for."

I blinked at him. "Does he really have that much money?"

Daniel's eyebrows lifted. "Look around. It might not all be from his books. Maybe he has family money. If he does, he's never disclosed it. Not that he would."

"This is insane," I murmured to myself. "Are we safe here?"

Hardy let out a heavy sigh. "I doubt Max would want to bring even more attention to himself. He knows our background, and I believe he hopes we'll solve this for him without bringing anyone else into it."

A thought occurred to me. "That's why Kevin was hinting around about it. His hands are tied."

"Bingo," Hardy said. "That poor guy. I can't imagine working in a police force where you have no power."

"No power when it comes to Max," Daniel said. "He's only one man and protects his interests."

I stared at him for a long moment. "The Me-Too movement went viral because of just one man."

Hardy gently squeezed my shoulders.

"I'm not justifying anything, Dakota. Please don't take it that way. What I'm saying is Max has no skin in the game for anything else going on in this town. I think it's safe to say the police can do whatever they want as long as they keep out of his affairs."

I grimaced. "I'm not sure that makes it better."

"It doesn't," Hardy said.

We walked for a little while, each lost in our own thoughts before coming upon a large stone greenhouse. An older woman stood at the door watering a flowering bush. When she saw us, she squinted and raised her hand up to shield her eyes.

"Hello!" she called. "You're far from the main house. Are you lost?"

Hardy nudged me.

"No, ma'am!" I called back. "We're exploring the grounds." I came closer and stuck my hand out. "I'm Dakota. This is my fiancé, Hardy, and our friend Daniel."

She eyed us all, but her gaze lingered on Daniel. "You look familiar. Do I know you?"

Daniel gave her a charming smile. "Not in person, but you might have seen my face in the back of my books."

The woman's eyes narrowed. "No. That's not it."

I pressed my lips together to keep from smiling.

"Did you date Daisy? You weren't the one who knocked her up and ran were you?"

Daniel gaped like a fish.

Hardy turned and coughed.

Daniel's mouth opened and closed. His ears turned crimson. "Err. No. I assure you I am most certainly not that man."

The woman shrugged. "Eh. My sight's not what it used to be, but you sure do look like him."

"Uh," Daniel said. "I have no idea who Daisy is."

"I've heard a few people say that when it comes to our Daisy." The woman nodded and poured the last of the water on the flowers. "Where are you from?"

Hardy spoke then. I think Daniel and I were too stunned to form words. They chatted briefly, then the woman opened the greenhouse door.

"I usually don't allow tourists inside, but you seem like nice people."

"Even him?" I asked, jerking a thumb at Daniel.

"Dakota," he hissed.

"Even the degenerate," the woman said.

I couldn't hold my laughter in this time.

The woman's name was Kathy. She'd worked on the grounds for over thirty years and knew Max as a child.

"He grew up spoiled," the woman said. "And he never grew out of it."

"Kathy, did you see any police or ambulance here yesterday evening?" Hardy asked.

The woman snorted. "Course I did. My vision might

be poor, but I'm not dumb. I came in to grab some things from the kitchen and saw them all going in Max's side door. The one he never lets any of us use."

"Who uses it?" I asked.

Kathy gave us a suspicious look. "Why so curious?"

Hardy gave me a warning look. "Miss Kathy, someone was hurt on the premises last night and no one in the house seems to know about it except for Max."

Kathy waved a hand. "Of course they don't. That man has more secrets than an Egyptian tomb. He's a tough nut to crack." She peered up at Hardy. "Is that person okay?"

Daniel winced.

Hardy crouched down on one knee so he was eye level with Kathy, who'd taken a seat at the potting table. "I'm afraid not."

"Oh. Well, that's a shame, isn't it? Was her family with her?"

"We don't know. Right now, we have few answers but a lot of questions."

Kathy patted the last bit of dirt around a pothos into a small temporary pot and set it aside before grabbing another pot and doing the same thing with another. "You should start with the waitstaff," she advised. "They see and hear everything. Max pays them well, and they've learned to keep their mouth shut."

On the surface, Kathy seemed a little kooky, but on a closer look, I noticed a spark there. She was enjoying this. Chatty Kathy might not be crazy or half blind after all.

"Where are they during the day?" Hardy asked.

Kathy shrugged. "Here. There. Max keeps quarters for them on the lower level."

Hardy grinned at the woman, and a pink blush colored her cheeks. He reached over and patted her hand. "You've been helpful today, Kathy. How about we come to visit you again soon?"

Her mouth fell open, and it took her a moment to speak. That ol' Cavanaugh charm had rendered the poor woman speechless. "Uh. Yes." She let out a girlish giggle. "That would be wonderful."

Hardy rose and held out his hand to help Kathy up. Her blush deepened as he helped her rise. She reached over and took one of the pothos she'd potted. "Here." Kathy pressed it into his hands. "For you."

"Thank you," Hardy said. "I'll take great care of it."

Kathy smiled, her brown eyes twinkling.

"Come on, Casanova," I murmured, taking him by the elbow.

Hardy winked at me. "Bye, Miss Kathy."

She waved. "Bye, Hardy. Don't forget your promise."

He laid a hand over his heart. "I would never."

Daniel rolled his eyes and headed out of the greenhouse.

When we were outside, he clapped Hardy on the back. "Still have that charm, Hardy. Even with the senior citizens."

"If it works, it works." Hardy snagged me around the waist and kissed my neck.

"If it solves this murder, he can play Romeo all he

wants." I steered us deeper into the property. With no witnesses and no real evidence, we had very little to go on. But even worse than that, a murderer still roamed the mansion, and we had no idea who it was.

If we didn't solve this thing fast, that poor woman might not be the only victim.

EIGHT

We wandered back to the mansion later than I liked, just in time for lunch. Everyone gathered in the same room where breakfast was served. Hardy and I sat in different seats this time, closer to the front of the room, where we got a good view of everyone.

Daniel made his excuses and wandered upstairs. He had that faraway look in his eyes when a new scene popped into his head, and I knew whatever I said would fall on deaf ears.

I leaned over. "We're going about this the wrong way."

Hardy nodded. "I think so too. Any thoughts about how to re-right the ship?"

An idea had been percolating in my head all morning. "We all signed an NDA."

"I can't remember what it says, but yes."

My mind whirled with possibility. "We aren't allowed

to speak of the details of this event. No negative social media postings."

A slow grin curved Hardy's lips. "And no discussion of any events that went on inside the house once we leave."

"Under the terms of the agreement, we can technically tell everyone there was a murder, as long as we don't discuss it once we leave."

Hardy let out a wicked chuckle. "I love your devious brain."

"When we're finished, let's read through it one more time and let Quinn do the same. If we all agree, I think dinner is a great time to bring it up, don't you think?"

He laced his fingers with mine underneath the table. "Working with you is always a delight, Dakota."

LUNCH PASSED WITH LITTLE FANFARE. Everyone had found their own little group of people to hang out with. Quinn was already in the room when we arrived. Poppy hopped off the bed and came running toward me, twining in and out of my legs. I scooped her up and snuggled her.

"I missed you!"

Poppy meowed.

"Fang is okay?" I asked Quinn.

He rolled his eyes. "If you mean being a holy terror, then yes, he's fine."

Hardy barked a laugh.

Quinn gave him an exasperated look. "Harper goes in

the morning, and I go in the afternoon. He's well fed and well entertained."

Fang was a ball of frenetic energy. We thought about buying him the cat version of a flirt pole to help him work some of that energy out, but we hadn't done it yet. The small ones worked, but I thought that if we could get him outside and really get him to chase that pole for a little, he'd collapse in a heap of happy exhaustion instead of leaping out from corners at us all hours of the day.

Poppy, on the other hand, enjoyed being lazy. After months of trying to initiate play time and her giving me the cat equivalent of an eye roll, I started waiting for her to give me the cue to play. Otherwise, all I was doing was wasting time and energy trying to engage her in a game she didn't want to play.

I sat on a chair and curled Poppy into my chest. "Did anyone see you come in?"

"The weird butler dude. He seemed taken aback by the cat, but when I told him who I was, he led me up here and left." Quinn snickered. "He came back half an hour later with a bag of cat food and told me to do my best to keep the cat contained."

We all laughed. Fat chance of that happening. Poppy went where she wanted when she wanted to. If she didn't want to be found, no one would find her.

The cat purred contentedly as if she agreed. I hadn't noticed any other animals on the grounds, but that didn't mean there wasn't another feline prowling around the place. "Maybe Poppy can help us find some clues since we're coming up with nothing."

Quinn shook his head in bemusement. "I can't believe you think your cat helps you solve murders."

"I don't think that. I know it." It sounded insane, but several times over the years, Poppy had been in the right place at the right time or led me to discover something that turned a case on its ear. Whether she knew what she was doing...well, that wasn't up to me, and I didn't want to dive too deep into things. I wasn't one for the supernatural, and Poppy's odd skill of finding things I needed at the exact right moment seemed to veer into that territory.

Examining it too much might ruin it, so I wouldn't look this particular gift horse (or cat) in the mouth. Hardy reached over and scratched Poppy on the head. "As strange as it sounds, I agree with Dakota. There's something odd about her cat."

"Not odd," I huffed. "Wonderful."

Poppy ignored us all and had fallen asleep against me.

"She hates the cat carrier by the way," Quinn said, nudging it with his foot. "You may need a new one."

I glanced down and winced at the shredded inside. "She could have ridden without it."

Quinn shook his head. "Uh uh," he said vehemently. "I was not going to risk losing your cat somewhere in the wilderness."

I waved a hand at him in dismissal. "Poppy knows where the blankets and snacks are. No way she's going to run off to hunt on her own."

A knock on the door interrupted our banter. Hardy turned, his brow furrowing. "Are you expecting anyone?"

Quinn and I shook our heads.

"Stay out of sight." Hardy walked over to the door and peeked out the peephole. His hand rested at his waist where he'd normally have a gun. Old habits died hard.

"It's Kevin," he said and opened the door.

The officer was alone this time. Hardy allowed him entrance, and he stopped when he saw the cat and Quinn.

"Am I interrupting something?" Kevin's eyes landed on Poppy and stayed.

"Not at all. If I'm stuck here, I want the comforts of home." I smiled. "Have a seat if you can find a place."

"No need. I won't take up too much of your time." He leaned against the desk. "You must be Quinn." He nodded.

Quinn rose and offered his hand. "That's right. Thanks for getting me in."

They shook. "It was a joint effort. Though the cat was a weird ask." Kevin shook his head. "Max doesn't have any pets in the house."

"I'm not sure I trust people who don't have any pets," I grumbled halfheartedly.

Quinn jerked his head at me. "Dakota's request. I try not to ask questions. I usually don't want to hear the answers."

The men shared a conspiratorial laugh that made me squirm. I wasn't that bad. "Kevin?" I asked.

"Yes, Miss Dakota?"

"Is there a reason you haven't asked anyone any questions? Aren't you supposed to interview everyone?"

Kevin's eyes flashed. "Normally we do, yes."

My eyebrows rose when he didn't answer my question.

Kevin sighed and crossed his arms. "I think we all know why we didn't."

Hardy and Quinn exchanged meaningful looks.

"I'd change it if I could, but he's the largest donor we have. My hands are tied."

"Is the entire city under his thumb?" Quinn asked.

Kevin's lips tightened. "You'll make it worse for us if you call attention to this," he warned.

"At first, maybe," Quinn acknowledged. "But wouldn't you want to work for someone who is on the right side of the law?"

The officer snorted. "There's always some bigger chump with a fat wallet waiting in the wings. You know it. I know it. Everyone knows it. We might get a reprieve, but five years down the road, we'll be in the same boat we were before all this."

"The devil you know," Hardy said quietly.

"Exactly. But Max is the reason I am here. He doesn't want us questioning his guests, but you can."

I frowned. "I'm sure he doesn't want anyone questioning them."

"Yes, but you're paying guests and not on his payroll." Kevin smiled hopefully. "There's nothing to lose."

"Uh huh. With as much money as Max seems to have, you don't think he can make a phone call and make our lives more difficult?" It took a lot not to roll my eyes at him. This guy wanted us to do his job for him. Granted, it wasn't about that. A woman was dead and so far, there were zero leads.

Kevin's lips tightened. "I have to work in this town every single day. I'm doing the best I can with what I have."

"Hmmm." I was judging him, but I couldn't help myself. Even if I lost my job, I would probably do the right thing. There would always be other jobs out there.

He pushed away from the desk. "Look, Max will throw me out if he sees me questioning anyone. He's all about the perception of things, especially when it comes to his reputation. Think about it. That's all I'm asking."

We already were thinking about it, but I didn't tell him that. Instead, I nodded, and Kevin let himself out.

"You were hard on him," Hardy observed.

"He deserved it."

Quinn's lips twitched. "Agreed, but I know what it's like dealing with someone like that. Max has all the power and Kevin has none."

"We have the legal system!" I snapped.

"And it's bought and paid for by Max Steinhoffer," Hardy said. He sighed and rubbed a hand over his face. "Let's take a look at the NDA and make sure we can't get sued. If we're clear, we need to make a plan for dinner tonight." His blue eyes softened. "Things like this are happening all over the world, Dakota. Kevin has a family to feed. We're extremely fortunate that we have a large nest egg. If something happens to us, we'll be okay. Other people might be living paycheck to paycheck. It's not up to us to judge. Whether we like it or not, sometimes doing the right thing comes at too high of a cost."

Silence fell in the room. I opened my mouth to respond hotly but took a deep breath instead and mulled his words. It pained me to realize he was right. Maybe I was too rigid sometimes. But this seemed egregious. A woman may not get justice because some rich blowhard doesn't want bad publicity.

Breathe, Dakota. I inhaled and exhaled a couple of times before I could speak. "You're right."

Quinn coughed. I shot him a hot glare. He ducked his head to hide a smile.

Jerk.

"If Kevin's hands are tied, then we should be the ones to try to get justice for this poor girl." I snapped my fingers. "I forgot to ask if they identified her yet."

Hardy pulled out his cell. "I'll ask. Want to grab the NDA?"

I stood and carried Poppy to her bed, gently laying her inside before digging inside my purse for the small manila folder with all our documents about this trip. Once I had it and some pens and highlighters, I headed to the small round table and spread everything out. Quinn and Hardy pulled up chairs, and we each took a turn reading over everything.

Someone knocked on the door again. Daniel this time. He squeezed in between me and Hardy, also taking a turn reading over everything. When the document finished making the rounds, we sat back and stared at each other. Slow smiles crept over everyone's face.

"We got him, don't we?" I said, breathless with excitement.

"I think we do," Quinn agreed. "Max's lawyers thought of most things, but murder rarely comes to mind when drafting an NDA." He stretched and laced his hands behind his head. "So, what do we do?"

Daniel grinned. "We start with good old-fashioned gossip and see where it takes us."

NINE

Mary and Heath had a much larger room than we did, so big it had a separate living area with a fireplace and a large round coffee table, along with bookshelves crammed with hardcovers and paperbacks. Heavy maroon curtains hung over the windows, pulled to the side with embroidered golden ropes tied in a neat bow. The last of the day's light trickled in, casting a glow upon everything.

Two oil lamps flickered with flame on top of the fireplace. I glanced at Hardy only to see him scanning the place. The couple sat on a large golden couch, dressed to the nines. Mary wore a golden sheath dress glittering with sequins and nude heels. Her pale skin was smooth, a slight sheen on her legs from lotion. Or maybe that was the way über wealthy people looked. No idea.

Heath wore a tan suit with a crisp white button-down shirt and navy pants. Sharp, shiny loafers completed his look. I admired his willingness to drink red wine and wear white. That took nerves of steel.

I'd worn a navy blue dress and nude pumps with a tan cashmere cardigan, one of my few luxury purchases since selling the Audubon book. There was something about cashmere that made me want to cover my entire house in it and roll around in luxury. Since that would be weird, I settled on the occasional luxury buy.

Normally, I bought items like this second hand. eBay was my go-to, but a few other great sites had popped up with some quality items I was keeping an eye on. Even now, I struggled to fully grasp that I could buy whatever I wanted whenever I wanted.

The cashmere cardigan was the first step.

When it came to Izzy, though? I winced internally. I bought that adorable little girl whatever she wanted. Within reason. It was a weakness. Balancing a mother's duty to keep her child grounded and the desire to give that child everything you never had was a dangerous tightrope. Fortunately, I was still walking it successfully, but she was still young. I shuddered to think how expensive a teenage girl was.

Izzy wasn't mine, but we'd claimed each other, and that was good enough for me.

Hardy wore charcoal slacks and a deep blue button-down shirt with a casual blazer. The shirt brought out the stunning sapphire color of his eyes and offset the golden undertone of his skin. Every time I looked at him my breath caught, and all I could think about was how lucky I was to have him.

Hardy squeezed my fingers. I dropped my eyes and smiled.

Mary and Heath stood. "Welcome! The others will be here in just a little while. Please have a seat." Her brow furrowed. "You didn't bring your charming companion?"

I frowned. "Companion?" Was she talking about my cat? Mary didn't seem like the type of person to enjoy animals, but I could be mistaken.

"That dark-haired author. What was his name again?"

Hardy's soft snort almost made me laugh. "Ah. Daniel Jensen. Would you like us to let him know? I didn't realize you'd included him in the invite otherwise I would have asked him."

Mary beamed. "Please do!"

Hardy pulled out his cell and texted Daniel. "He said he had some writing to do, so he may not show."

"That's no problem." Mary smiled graciously and sat back down with her husband. "Now, let me tell you about our wines."

HALF AN HOUR LATER, I wanted to scream. Now, I liked wine. I liked the pretty bottles. I liked certain grapes. Certain flavors, certain blends, etc. What I had no idea I didn't like until this very moment was long-winded explanations in excruciating detail about how a particular wine was made. What type of wood they used for the barrel, the temp in the storage facility, sulfite vs no sulfite, the grapes, the care of the grapes...

I half expected Hardy to slide off the loveseat in a stupor. Daniel, bless his occasionally stuffy heart, either had a Masters' degree in Charm, or this dork enjoyed every single second of it. He'd not only shown up, he'd taken the time to put on a pair of slacks and a blazer, all black of course, and a crisp lavender-colored shirt, and had, from the second he'd walked in, almost charmed the gold fillings right out of Mary James' teeth.

It was horrifying, really, but also very, very impressive. Mr. James, on the other hand, was far less impressed with Daniel than Mary and had a little bit of jealous insecurity going on. He occasionally interjected something into the conversation using huge words that didn't always fit. Embarrassment for him made me squirm.

Hardy and I barely said two words since Daniel walked in. We didn't have to. All we had to do was watch this train wreck in über-slow motion and see who was still standing at the end of it.

But then, as it usually did when Daniel got involved, things got interesting. Mary poured us all another glass of wine—this one from oak barrels bought from some shaman in the Andes. Or something. Who knows? Daniel leaned in, eyes sparkling. "Say, I heard something very interesting today."

I almost rubbed my hands together like a cartoon villain. Here we go!

"Oh?" Mary leaned in so close their noses almost

BOOK CLUB BAIT & SWITCH   75

touched. Heath's cheeks reddened, and rage flickered in his eyes.

I discreetly scooted my foot over and tapped the top of Daniel's shoe to warn him to tone it down some before there was a brawl. Daniel leaned back in his chair, a smile lifting the edges of his lips. "Someone said the police and ambulance were here last night, and they pulled a body from Max's extra library."

Mary gasped, her hand fluttering to her chest. "My heavens!" She turned to her husband. "Heath! Did you hear that?"

"I'm sitting right here, darling," Heath gritted. "Of course, I heard him."

I pressed my lips together.

"Well, who was it?" Mary asked Daniel.

He shrugged. "No idea. All I know was she was young, and it sounded like she was involved in an affair with someone here at the event."

Mary's eyes widened. Her cheeks were flushed pink with excitement. "An affair!"

Daniel nodded. "Do you have any idea who it could be?"

Heath glared at Daniel. "We shouldn't speculate about that woman's business," he snapped.

Daniel lifted his shoulder in a casual shrug. "Considering we all might be staying with a murderer, I think we'd do ourselves a disservice if we didn't, don't you think?"

Heath blinked in surprise. "Well, I—" he paused. "I guess I didn't think of it that way."

Mary reached over and patted his thigh. "Maybe we should have more people in for wine and see what we can find out."

I frowned. "Wasn't there supposed to be another couple here?"

Mary's lips turned down. "Yes, there was. I'd forgotten about it!" She chuckled ruefully. "I get so excited talking about wine, I lose hours sometimes!"

Hours? Goodness. I thought half an hour was painful. I would have melted into a puddle of boredom right onto the floor if she'd gone on much longer about her Pinot Noir.

"Should we make sure they're okay?"

Heath snorted derisively. "They're adults. I'm sure everything is fine."

Daniel made a noise that made Heath let out a long-suffering sigh. "You don't agree?"

"If there's a murderer among us, checking on them is better safe than sorry, don't you think?"

Mary reached over and patted her husband's hand. "He's right, Heath. Why don't you send them a text?"

Heath looked like he wanted to chew on cement but dutifully pulled his phone out to send a message.

It buzzed almost right away. He glanced down. "They're fine. Says they got caught up chatting about tax havens with one of the other couples."

Was this what it was like to be rich—where talking about taxes was more entertaining than mooching free

BOOK CLUB BAIT & SWITCH   77

wine off of strangers? If it was, I was doing wealthy very wrong.

But I didn't want to change a thing. Hardy tapped me on the thigh. "I think we should freshen up for dinner. You want to head back to the room?"

I nodded. "Yes, of course. Daniel? You coming?"

"Oh!" Mary exclaimed. "You don't all have to leave!"

All being Daniel. I hid my smile and watched Daniel's expression as he tried to figure out what to say.

"As much as I've loved this, I, too, need to freshen up. I came right out of a long writing session and need to clean up the workspace and put on a fresh shirt for dinner."

Her look of disappointment made Hardy turn away. Maybe Daniel was in the wrong career field. If he could easily charm someone like Mary, our investigations would go much easier with him around.

"I'd love to do this again, though."

Mary beamed at him. Heath grunted.

"Heath," Daniel said. "It was a pleasure to chat with you."

Heath just stared at him.

We waited until we were far out of earshot before laughing ourselves breathless.

"That was exhausting," Daniel muttered.

"You're pretty good at pretending," I said.

"Most introverts are. We'd never get anywhere in society if we showed everyone how much of a troll we really are."

"I think I'm the biggest troll here," I said dryly as we

stepped into our room. "If I have to put real pants on one more time during this vacation, I might scream."

"You wear real pants to work every day," Daniel observed.

"Nope. I wear stretchy pants that look like real pants. Unfortunately, everyone here is rich and judgmental, so I made the right call in bringing pants with zippers."

Hardy shook his head in amusement.

Quinn turned and greeted us.

"Everything good here?" Hardy asked.

"I put listening devices in Max's study and library."

I sucked in a breath. "Whoa. Risky."

Quinn's eyes twinkled. "Former FBI, darling. We're sneaky like that."

"Interesting," Daniel said. "If you hear what he's working on next, mind letting me know?"

I smacked Daniel's arm. "Don't be a cheater."

He laid a hand over his heart, and his eyes widened in mock shock. "Not a cheater, merely curious. We don't even write in the same genre. You do misjudge me sometimes, Dakota."

Quinn closed the folder he was working on. "No can do. This is solely for our investigation." He tapped his pen on the desk. "Oh, and I figured out who the victim was."

Hardy frowned. "Kevin never responded to me."

"That's because he called while you were gone and set up some kind of messaging system." Quinn tapped a few keys on his laptop and turned the screen around. "Apparently, he thinks texts and calls here are too risky."

Hardy and I exchanged a glance. "You think he's monitoring everything?"

"Couldn't tell you. I'm a little techy—enough to set up devices, but when it comes to the deep dive stuff, I'm a complete neophyte. It's not one of my skill sets."

I nudged Hardy. "That's what we need. One of those jack-of-all-trade computer geek people. They'd love this."

"Maybe we can look into it when we get back." His brow furrowed. "Isn't there a couple who works in tech here?"

"Kristy and David," Daniel said. "But we can't ask for their help just in case they're in on it."

Hardy rubbed his chin. "Good point. Who was the victim?"

Quinn peered at his notes. "Angela Baker. 27. Unmarried, no children. She worked as a teacher's aide at the local junior high. I'm waiting on a more detailed background check."

"Nothing about links to anyone here?" Hardy asked.

"None so far."

Daniel checked the time on his phone. "It's been fifteen minutes. How many people do you think know about the murder by now?"

Quinn laughed. "Planted the first seed tonight?"

"Daniel practically charmed the pants right off Mary this evening," I said ruefully.

Daniel gave a little bow. "I'll see you at dinner. I really do need to put the final touches on some things." With that, he left the room.

Dinner was in forty-five minutes. Not enough time to take a nap, but enough time to mourn not taking one. "Want us to bring you back a plate?" I asked Quinn.

"Nah. I hit it off with one of the kitchen staff earlier, and I have a casual date set up."

I blinked. "A...what?"

Quinn grinned at my befuddled look. "She's a cute server, and I'm a hungry guy."

A lot could change in a year. When I first met him, Quinn was undercover at a speed dating event, still grieving the loss of his wife. Even now, he didn't date much, but he was a lot more casual about the possibility.

"Good for you," I said after a long moment. "Are you going to ask her about Angela?"

"What kind of employee would I be if I didn't? I'm a multitasker. A good meal and an info gathering session are two of my favorite things."

Hardy shrugged off his jacket and hopped onto the bed. "We'll see what kind of damage we can do at the main dinner. If Max is there, we may need to tread carefully."

Good point. "Agreed. But I suspect the gossip mill is in full effect if Mary has anything to say about it." I kicked off my shoes and slid in beside him.

Quinn rolled his eyes. "Don't do anything weird, please."

I wiggled my eyebrows at him. "My middle name is weird."

"I'm well aware," he said dryly.

Poppy scooted out from under a chair and leaped onto

the bed with us, turning in a few circles before she curled up next to me.

"See? She's not worried about it." I stroked a hand down Poppy's silk fur.

"That's the first time I've seen that cat all day." Quinn frowned. "There's no way she's been there the entire time."

"She can disappear when she wants to." There had been numerous times I'd lost her in the store and spent way too long trying to find her.

"By the way," he said, "Harper called earlier. Everything at the store is fine, but she said you had a few people show up for the investigative side."

"If we get this taken care of, we'll be home in a few days. Did she happen to get their info?"

Quinn waved his cell at me. "I have it right here. Want me to call everyone back?"

"If you have time. Technically, we're on vacation." Word of mouth had picked up business substantially over the last year. Now we had the occasional walk-in, as well as phone calls and emails. Hardy and I were still on the fence about our future and what direction we might go once we were married. Izzy was in a good place with school and new friends, and Harper all but ran the store in my absence. We could take the P.I. business anywhere, but we both loved living in the town we were in now. But we also felt there was something more out there for us.

To be honest, my priorities had changed since getting serious with Hardy. I no longer wanted the same things I used to, and the danger this business could bring no longer brought the same thrill. Once Izzy barreled into my life, I realized that little girl brought all the adventure one person could handle. Now that Hardy was a partner in the business and he faced the same dangers I did, I was forced to confront an uncomfortable truth.

I couldn't stand it when Hardy put himself in the line of fire, especially now that Izzy was in our lives. We didn't take too many dangerous cases anymore, but every once in a while, something like this came along.

Neither of us had to work, but both of us liked to. Was this P.I. business meant for the long-term for us, or could we figure out something else to keep us out of the thick of it but still allow us to help people?

We both had a lot of thinking to do.

Hardy groaned. "Dinner in twenty. Should we walk down?"

I buried my face in his chest. "No."

His chest rumbled with amusement. "Neither of us has dates with cute kitchen staff, so this is the only way we can eat. Plus, we need to rile up the masses and see who breaks first."

I sighed and flopped onto my back. Poppy lifted her head and gave me a baleful stare. "Sorry, kitty. We gotta go. Quinn will keep you entertained."

"I'll do no such thing," Quinn protested.

"Don't listen to that grumpy Gus," I murmured in her fur as I dropped a kiss on top of her head.

Quinn turned his attention back to his laptop. "Have

fun, kids. Let's plan to meet back here in two hours. Is that enough time?"

"Plenty," Hardy said.

With a noise of protest, I rolled off the bed and into a standing position, brushing out the wrinkles in my cardigan. Hardy followed, and after a few minutes of refreshing ourselves, we headed back into the hallway and toward dinner.

TEN

Vacation was weird. You woke up, ate, explored, then ate again, maybe took a break, then ate one more time. Everything revolved around food, and it was kind of exhausting.

Here we were again. Seated at the same place as last time and on our third course. I'd never thought about food more in my entire life.

Max had elected to take dinner in his own quarters, leaving Hardy and me the perfect opportunity to shake things up a bit. Daniel, like always, had made himself popular in a matter of minutes. He had most of the table laughing after telling an amusing anecdote about one of his signings. He sat beside me, close enough I could smell the cedar undernote of his cologne.

But as it turned out, there was no need for us to do anything.

Just as the last server disappeared through the door

after delivering the fourth course, Mary blurted out, "Did you hear there was a murder?"

Someone's spoon clattered to their plate. Dead silence fell in the room.

Daniel nudged my foot.

Everyone looked at each other, various expressions of shock and concern on their faces. Mary was enjoying the moment far too much. "I heard she was having an affair with someone in this very room!"

Several gasps sounded. The men all looked at each other, brows furrowed, as if trying to figure out who the guilty party was. I watched each of them carefully, but no one jumped out of their seat to exclaim it was them, unfortunately.

"Where are the police?" Kristy, the tech lady, asked.

"Max paid them off," Daniel drawled.

I stilled. "Daniel," I hissed under my breath.

"What? It's true."

"Yes, but maybe we shouldn't say things like that to people who know him."

Heath waved a hand. "No need to spare anyone's feelings. Not a single person in this room is surprised by that. In fact, I'm sure some of us sitting here have done it before." He let out a jovial laugh, and almost everyone else followed.

That dismissive, callous sound turned my stomach. Next to me, Hardy shifted uncomfortably.

"Come on, Dakota," Heath said. "Don't look so glum about it. That's the way the world works."

I gave him a polite smile. If that's the way the world worked, I didn't want any part of it.

"Power belongs to those who take it," someone else said. Richard. The one who wouldn't disclose what kind of business he had.

Samantha, the baker, gasped in horror. "You should all be ashamed of yourselves!"

The only couple who hadn't said a word was Mike and his wife, Sarah, the ones who were Max's friends. Word of this would get back to Max immediately. Of that, I had no doubt.

"So, who do we think it is?" Hailey said. Richard's wife and dressed to the nines, she wore a pinched expression that seemed permanent.

"The girl or the murderer?" Heath said jovially. He seemed to be in a much better mood than he was less than an hour ago, even with Daniel's presence in the room.

"I think the murderer's identity is more important at this time," Mary said dryly.

"It certainly isn't us!" Wendy, the one who claimed her Chihuahua as her child, exclaimed.

"Mmmm. The first one to deny is usually the culprit," Richard said. His eyes twinkled as he said the words, as if this were all one big game.

"Maybe we should all start by disclosing our whereabouts last night," I said before this could go downhill any further.

"Where were you?" Mike asked.

I didn't want them to know I was the one who discovered the body, so I tiptoed around my answer.

"I was on the grounds exploring the garden," I said simply.

"Did you see anything?" Samantha asked, her words halting.

"The only thing I saw were those stunning purple pansies blooming outside," I said with an apologetic smile. "Right when I came back in, I spotted red and blue lights, but I didn't think much of it."

Hardy squeezed my knee gently. We hadn't planned on me lying through my teeth, but I wanted the attention off me and onto everyone else.

"I thought I saw you go into the library," Mike said slowly.

The new author gave me a curious stare.

"I did," I admitted, "but I didn't stay long. They have a quirky gardener on the premises who takes wonderful care of the landscaping. She has floods of gorgeous flowers blooming around the grounds right now." The part about the pansies wasn't a lie. She kept them in baskets and put them out each day just to keep the place from looking a little too dreary during winter.

Samantha smiled. "I may need to go see for myself. Sounds stunning."

"I'm happy to walk with you if you want to go after dinner," I offered.

"Be careful," Heath sang. "She might be the murderer."

Hardy stiffened beside me.

"Samantha can always bring someone with her if she's uncomfortable," I said with a tight smile. "But I think I'd be more careful hanging out with you alone."

Heath blustered, his face reddening.

Mary laid a hand on his arm and sent me a quelling look. "She's just trying to get a rise out of you, darling."

I let a slow smile cross my face. Heath flinched.

Mary shook her head. "Heath and I were in our room on a video call with our daughter. I'm happy to give the police her phone number."

Samantha chimed in. "I snuck into the kitchen to check out their baking equipment." Her cheeks turned pink, and a sheepish smile crossed her face.

Nick's look turned doting. "That's my Sam," he said fondly. "There's never been a mixer she hasn't wanted to take home with her."

I noticed Nick didn't disclose where he was. "Books grab me the same way," I said.

"I'd love that walk later." Samantha held her wine glass up as the server passed by with the bottle.

"Of course. Hubbies or no hubbies?"

She laughed. "How about a girls' walk first?"

"Done." I tilted my wine glass in a salute.

The conversation turned to different things for a while, but I could hear the occasional murmured whisper about what happened, mixed with speculation over who could have done it. I spent the rest of the dinner trying to make small talk while keeping an ear open for anything interesting.

WHEN DINNER FINISHED, I went upstairs to change my shoes and get my jacket, then headed out the back with Samantha.

Sam shivered. "Maybe I should have brought my hat."

"I don't expect we will be out long. It's far too cold to admire the pansies for too long."

We shared a smile and took the stone path toward the back.

"This place is something else," Sam said quietly. "I've never been in a place this grand. Have you?"

"Not quite like this," I admitted. "Daniel is well known in the crime fiction world, so he has an estate, but this is..." I tried to think of the right way to describe it. "A monstrosity," I finally said.

She barked a laugh. "That's a good word. Doesn't Max live alone?"

"As far as I know. Some of the staff live on the grounds, though. The kitchen staff is downstairs, I think. The gardener lives in a cottage on the land. I'm sure there are others. He must have a few hundred acres out here."

Samantha nodded. "At least." She tugged her sweater closer. "How is it owning a bookstore?"

"Amazing," I admitted. "It's a wonderful feeling to work in the field you love."

Sam's eyes crinkled at the edges when she smiled. "I agree. Where I come from, food is love. There's nothing like seeing someone's eyes light up when you hand them a slice of chocolate cake or a piece of apple pie still warm from the oven."

We rounded the corner close to the greenhouse. Sam gaped at the baskets of overflowing flowers.

"I think she pulls them in every night."

"She must. It's far too cold to keep them out. I'm surprised they're out this late. The temp must be in the 20s."

I frowned. That was odd. Kathy seemed obsessed with the plants in the greenhouse. "Stay back," I said quietly, pulling out my cell phone to turn on the flashlight.

"Dakota?" Sam's voice quavered. "Is everything okay?"

I knocked on the greenhouse door. "Kathy?" I called.

No answer.

I knocked again. When no one answered, I tried to push my way in, only to feel resistance on the other side. I pushed harder. "Kathy?"

"Dakota?" Samantha said again.

I held up a hand. "Hold on."

"Kathy? Can you hear me? It's Dakota from earlier. Are you okay?"

A soft exhalation of air came from inside. Crouching down, I stuck my arm inside and felt around. There. Something soft and warm.

"Help."

I scrambled back and sent a quick text to Hardy.

Greenhouse. Help. Now.

"Samantha, can you see if there's a back way in?"

"Uh. Of course." The sound of her footsteps faded as she ran around the other side.

"I'm here, Miss Kathy," I said. "Hold on."

"Dakota!" Samantha shouted. "I found it!"

I followed the sound of her voice, finding her standing at the side door.

"Here," she said. "It's locked."

I double checked the door knob, shoving against it, but it held tight.

"Dakota!"

I spun. "Over here!"

Hardy appeared in view in seconds, with Daniel tagging along behind him.

Relief filled me when I saw his face. "Kathy is in there, and I think she's injured. Can you get this door open?"

Hardy lifted the flashlight, studied it for a moment, then took a few steps back. "Watch out."

I tugged Samantha away from the door as Hardy lifted his foot. Three kicks later, the door made a sickening crunch of noise, and Hardy was able to reach in and unlock the door.

He and Daniel rushed in.

"Kathy! We're coming," I called as I hurried in after them. Samantha stared at me with wide eyes, but didn't follow.

We found Kathy lying on her side, wedged against the bottom of the door. Hardy fell to his knees, reaching to take her pulse.

She moaned.

"Thank goodness," I breathed.

"Call an ambulance," Hardy said. "Someone hit her in the back of the head."

"What is the meaning of this!" a sharp male voice snapped from the back entrance.

"I got this," Daniel said quietly, turning to intercept Max.

I couldn't make out what they were saying, but Max sounded furious. He tried to get past Daniel twice, but Daniel managed to fend him off.

"You called the police!" Max shouted.

This guy...I took a deep breath and tried to ignore him.

Hardy stood and marched over to Max and Daniel. "Mr. Steinhoffer, your employee is gravely injured. Medical intervention is necessary to save her life."

Max snorted. "Nonsense. Just pick her up and put her to bed. She probably dipped a little too much into the whiskey and tripped over one of these godforsaken pots."

Hardy's jaw tightened. "I'm afraid someone attacked Kathy. She sustained a serious head wound."

"And I said she'll be fine!" Max took a step toward Hardy and stilled when my fiancé didn't move.

"Mr. Steinhoffer, are you telling me you are choosing your reputation over a human life?"

Max blinked. He opened his mouth, shut it, then looked at me and Daniel. "Of course not," he snapped.

"Good. The ambulance is on its way. My fiancée was first on the scene and will help the police file an official report."

Max scoffed. "There's no need for a police report. Kathy's fallen before. I keep telling her to clean things up in here."

Daniel shook his head. "You have no idea who you're dealing with." A rueful chuckle escaped him.

Hardy gave Max a long, flat stare. "I am a former detective with over twenty years' experience in my field. This was no accident." The sound of sirens screamed down the road.

Max's head snapped toward the noise. "I'm a private person. There's no need for anyone else to know what's happening on my property."

"If you don't want anyone to know, don't tell them," Hardy said dismissively. "In the meantime, Kathy needs to be transported to the hospital as soon as possible." He took a step closer to Max. "You might have money, but that means absolutely nothing to me or anyone standing here. I won't stand for someone trying to pressure me or my fiancée into lying for you."

Max turned red. "I should have you thrown out of here!"

Hardy shrugged. "Please do. I'd love nothing more than to leave all of you selfish, entitled people behind."

I ducked my head to hide my smile.

"How dare you—" Max began.

Daniel stepped in. "Max, cut the nonsense. Let Hardy and Dakota handle this and go back to your cushy little study and your words. This is ridiculous. You have someone in your home trying to silence people who might have helped them try to solve this murder, and you're throwing every roadblock you can at us."

Max gaped like a fish.

"One might wonder why you're so resistant to a police presence," Daniel continued, cocking his head in curiosity. "Are you hiding something?" A wicked smile tipped his lips up.

Max stared at Daniel before dropping his eyes. "Fine, but get them out of here as soon as possible." He turned and stalked from the greenhouse, his steps hurried.

Daniel watched him go, then turned to us. "I've known Max for a while, and he's normally an entitled jerk, but he's never been this unkind." He frowned. "Maybe we should look into him."

I shook my head. "Absolutely not. I could not care less about Max Steinhoffer. Hardy set this up so we could relax, and—"

"EMS!"

I let out a breath. "Back here!" I called.

Daniel reached over and patted my shoulder. "I know."

Two paramedics came through. Hardy engaged the first one in discussion, and Daniel and I stayed out of the way. Two police officers came a few minutes later and took my statement.

"Will she be all right?" I asked when the paramedics had Kathy strapped in and ready to transport.

The older one nodded. "I think so, but she'll need scans. Head wounds can be unpredictable." He gave me a polite smile and pushed the stretcher through the greenhouse and out the door.

The officers finished up with Hardy and started to head out.

I reached for one and stopped him. "Can you put an officer on her room?"

"Yes ma'am. We plan to take every precaution."

"Thank you."

He nodded and walked out, tucking his pen in his pocket as he went.

I leaned against the potting table and let out a long sigh. The room fell quiet, the sound of the police and medical personnel growing fainter as they left the scene.

"They're actually going to the house this time and asking questions," Hardy said.

"Why now?" I walked over and leaned against him.

Hardy put his arm around me. "Because I strongly suggested I would make their lives very difficult if they didn't."

I smiled, but it quickly faded. "Max is a jerk." He was more than that. He was a terrible person.

"I couldn't agree more," Hardy said. "Let me look around for a few minutes and we'll head back."

"They didn't do that already?" Daniel asked.

Hardy snorted. "A cursory search, if you could call it

96   S.E. BABIN

that. Even though they're going into the house doesn't mean they're taking it seriously. Baby steps."

"I'll help you look." The flashlight on my cell phone came in handy, and we'd just settled in to search the greenhouse when the sound of footsteps made me look up.

Samantha stood there watching. "Dakota? Do you have a moment?"

I dusted my hands off. "Sure. Everything okay?"

She jerked her head and turned to go outside.

Hardy watched her. "Be careful," he said in a low voice.

"Of course, but I don't think she's our culprit."

"You never know. It's always the quiet ones," Daniel said, but from his tone, I knew he was teasing.

Sam stood close to an oak tree, her hands shoved in her pockets.

I turned off the flashlight and hurried toward her. The temperature was dropping rapidly, and the cold was beginning to be uncomfortable.

"I wanted to tell you this before everything happened, but that woman was more important than this," Samantha said.

"Okay. What is it?"

She looked in all directions before lowering her voice. "Nick wasn't with me last night. I have no idea where he went."

My eyebrows hitched up. "Did you ask?"

Sarah looked down, scraping at the earth with the toe

of her boot. "No. I didn't want to know. But things are different with that girl getting killed."

I hesitated to ask, but it might help narrow the suspect list down. "Do you suspect he's having an affair?"

Samantha closed her eyes and let out a long breath. "I'm not sure. He's retired, so he doesn't really have a set schedule. Nick is busy most of the day, though. He plays golf or spends time with friends." She chewed on the side of her thumbnail. "If he really wanted to, it wouldn't be difficult."

"I'm sorry," I said quietly. "He might not be, but I think you need to ask. If only to make yourself feel better."

"Are you and Hardy really bookstore owners?"

I laughed. "Yes. My fiancé is former law enforcement, though." If anyone looked us up, they'd see we were private investigators, but for now I'd keep it mum.

Samantha's gaze trailed to the still flashing lights. "Is that woman going to be okay?"

"The paramedics said they think so. She has to do some tests, but once they get her in and treated, I believe she'll be okay."

She sagged against the tree trunk. "That's great news. What do you think happened?"

"Someone hit her on the back of the head. That's all I know."

"Terrible business." Samantha shook her head.

Hardy and Daniel walked out of the greenhouse. "Ready to head in?" my fiancé called.

"Ready?" I asked Sam.

"Never been more ready," she said with a laugh.

We fell into step close to one another and said our goodbyes when we made it inside.

Hardy put a hand out to stop me. He waited until Samantha disappeared from view. "I want to look at the library again," he said in a low voice.

"Did you find something?"

"Let's talk when we get back in the room."

Daniel's expression was grim. "I'm going back inside to see if I can chat anyone else up. The manuscript event is in two days, and it may be much harder to talk to anyone then. If we can get this cleared up by tomorrow, we can all get out of here." His smile was wan. "I'm caring less and less about the events and more about getting home and forgetting this ever happened."

"Ditto," I said quietly, linking my arm through Hardy's. "Ready?"

He pressed a kiss to the side of my temple. "Quiet and sneaky."

We parted ways with Daniel and had made our way halfway down the hall when a familiar orange striped cat stepped out of a side room and into our path. Poppy sat down and stared at us, her tail swishing like a cobra.

"Quinn is going to be so mad at you," I whispered to the cat as we got closer.

She stood, turned and swished her tail again, and ran to the entrance of the library.

"She's doing it again," Hardy murmured.

"You should be grateful. We've barely made any headway."

"Your cat is weird. You know that, right?"

I smiled. "Yup. She's also wonderful."

Poppy turned to stare at us, the look on her face one of barely concealed impatience.

"We're coming," I whispered.

Poppy darted inside.

ELEVEN

The house was quiet—the power of a police presence evident in the silent halls and rooms. Max was nowhere to be found, and I assumed he'd slunk back to his rooms after Daniel had shamed him.

Poppy kept looking back to ensure we were following her. We passed by the main study area first, but the cat had little interest in anything there. When we entered the second part of the library, Poppy didn't run off like I assumed she would. Instead, she padded over to where the victim had fallen and laid down. The area had already been thoroughly cleaned. Not a trace of the woman remained behind, and the room smelled like carpet shampoo.

Tears pricked the back of my eyes.

Hardy stopped in his tracks, his gaze steady on Poppy. Slowly, he shook his head. "I'll be darned."

I crouched down beside her and scratched her behind the ears. "Sweet cat."

She meowed plaintively.

A shuffling sound came from the doorway. "I knew that cat came after you." Quinn shook his head and stepped inside. "Have you found anything?"

"We just got here. How's the investigation going?"

Quinn snorted. "What investigation? They came in, asked a couple of questions, then released everyone." He rolled his eyes. "They all scattered like cockroaches when the lights came on."

"Let me guess," Hardy said. "No one knew anything?"

"Fresh and innocent as a newly bloomed daisy," Quinn said.

I scrubbed a hand over my face. "I hate this place."

Poppy meowed again.

"The cat agrees with you." Quinn looked around the room. "The cameras have yet to pick anything up. Whoever it was hasn't returned to the scene of the crime."

"Of course they haven't. That would make our job easier," I muttered.

Poppy rose from the floor, hurried over to Hardy, and whacked him several times with her paw.

Hardy looked down at Poppy, a gleam of amusement in his eyes. "Not here?"

Poppy meowed.

"We can't all be geniuses," Hardy said to her in exasperation.

I covered my mouth with my hand and turned away to hide my amusement. "What am I looking for?"

Hardy let out a sigh. "No idea. Anything that looks out of place. You witnessed the crime, so you're at an advantage. Do you remember what he wore?"

I frowned and thought back. "Dark pants and a blazer. Maybe blue, maybe black, maybe dark grey. The lighting is poor in here. Dark colors look the same."

"Any jewelry?"

I shook my head but paused. "A watch. Definitely gold. Right hand. I saw it when he turned to leave."

Hardy's head snapped up. "Are you sure?"

"About the gold or the hand?"

"Both."

"Yes. 100 percent."

Quinn and Hardy exchanged a look.

I glanced between them. "What?"

"Most people wear jewelry and watches on their non-dominant hand," Hardy said.

"That means he's left-handed?" If he was, the person would be significantly easier to find.

"Only ten percent of the population is left-handed," Quinn said. "But we can't take this as gospel. I know at least one person who wears their watch on their dominant hand. We can't jump to conclusions." He reached down and plucked something from the floor. "What we can do is keep an eye on everyone. It shouldn't be difficult to discover who favors their left hand."

"What if they're ambidextrous?" I asked.

Quinn and Hardy both stopped what they were doing. "Is she always like this?" Quinn asked.

"Every single day," Hardy said fondly.

"People can't help but use their dominant hand. He'll slip. I guarantee it," Quinn answered.

"As long as we're around to catch him when he does," I grumbled.

"Knowing our luck, the guy is saving all his left-hand time for playing guitar in his room," Hardy said under his breath.

"Meal times are when you'll catch him," Quinn said. "Eating is automatic. Look for someone hesitating when using their silverware or reaching for things."

Hardy moved to a new area and pushed a pile of books aside. Poppy meowed and swatted him on the leg again. He laughed and threw his hands up. "Fine. Show me the way, feline Lassie."

Poppy waited until Hardy straightened, then put her tail up and turned, leading him over to the almost hidden door to exit the room. With a shrug and an exasperated look toward us, he followed.

"Where did you get that cat?" Quinn asked.

"She came with the store."

He chuckled, but when I didn't laugh with him, he blinked in surprise. "Wait. You're serious?"

"Completely. The owner even put her in the contract." I smiled at the memory. "I'm contractually obligated to care for Poppy until the end of her days."

His chuckle deepened into a full-on guffaw. "That's

the strangest thing I've ever heard," he said when he caught his breath.

I had to laugh, too. It *was* weird. "She wouldn't leave the bookstore for the longest time. It took me a while to convince her the snacks are way better at my house than at the bookstore."

"Now she has a car hammock and a best friend."

"And a knack for solving murders, it seems," Hardy called. He held up something in his hand.

I squinted, trying to see what it was.

"A button?" Quinn asked.

"According to all the noise Poppy was making, this button belongs to our murderer." Hardy held it up to the light. It was a pale, creamy white.

"Umm. It looks like a button," I said helpfully.

Quinn reached for it and peered closely. "It's made of horn. Common in expensive suits, which we can assume everyone here is wearing. But not all high-end suit makers use bone."

"No one has worn the same thing twice since they've been here." Something in the corner by the wall where the woman fell caught my eye.

"It's a suit jacket," Hardy said. "Men aren't as particular as women about reusing clothing. We might see it again."

"Orrrrr," Quinn drawled. "We can enter some rooms and see what we can find."

I activated my flashlight as I bent down. A flash of shimmering white reflected back.

"An engagement ring," I breathed as I picked the diamond up. Warm light sent the diamond into brilliant refraction. "Who do you think this belongs to?"

"Could be the victim's." Hardy walked over and studied it before letting out a low whistle. "Beautiful ring. At least three carats. If it's hers, no wonder she was angry about being blown off."

I thought back to the argument I overheard between them. "When the man mentioned his wife, Angela commented on the woman not being his wife for much longer."

"That implies he told her he'd ask for a divorce." Hardy shook his head. "Typical. He was stringing her along."

"But he got her a ring." I tucked it into my pocket. "That's a big step."

Quinn grunted. "Not if he's as rich as the rest of these jokers. That's less than an hour's work for some."

"I wonder how many were born to it and how many are self-made." I shook my head and brushed away those thoughts. "Doesn't matter, I suppose. No matter where it comes from, money spends the same way."

"Ain't that the truth." Quinn straightened and groaned as he stretched. "I can't find anything else. You having any luck, Hardy?"

Poppy had flopped onto her back and was content swatting at the air. He nudged the cat with the toe of his loafer. "Not anymore. Seems our feline Agatha Christie is off duty."

I went over and scooped her up. "Good job."

She gently batted my face.

"Ready to go back to the room?"

Poppy meowed her agreement.

Quinn gave her a gruff head scratch. "Good job, cat."

I rolled my eyes at him. "Unlike you, she gets a midnight snack."

"Oh, Dakota," he lamented. "How you wound me."

Hardy chuckled and shut the door behind us as we left the library.

The mansion still held an unearthly silence, so we stayed silent, only speaking when we were back in our room.

"Did you bring a lockbox?" Hardy asked Quinn once we had kicked off our shoes and changed into more comfortable clothes.

Quinn reached into his briefcase and pulled out a thin, rectangular box. "Only a small one."

"It will work for these."

I dug out the ring and put it in the box. Hardy carefully wrapped the bone button in a small washcloth and did the same.

"Now," Quinn said with a wicked grin. "How are we going to break into everyone's rooms?"

TWELVE

I eyed him. "For a former FBI agent, you sure do like getting into trouble."

He lay on the second bed with his arms crossed behind his head, the picture of relaxation. "I couldn't do anything shady when I was in federal service. Now, the world is my oyster."

Hardy sighed. "The laws haven't suddenly gone away, Quinn."

"I know, but I don't represent the government anymore, so I have a much looser interpretation of those laws." He wiggled his eyebrows at me. "I heard Dakota got into a few pickles over the last couple of years, so don't go judging me."

I blushed. "Yes, but I didn't know the laws before I broke them," I said hotly.

"Not helping," Hardy said under his breath.

Quinn laughed. "Maybe I'll use that excuse one day."

My phone buzzed. Daniel.

Mind if I come up?

Bring wine?

Already in my hand.

I put my phone on the nightstand and pulled the blankets over my legs. "Daniel's coming up. He must have found something out."

"Let's hope," Quinn grumbled. "A button and a lost engagement ring do not make a slam dunk case." He sat up and opened his laptop, the sound of typing covering the silence.

Hardy came and sat down, picking my legs up to put them on his lap.

"Just got an email about Angela," Quinn said, frowning as he scrolled through the message.

"Anything interesting?" Hardy asked.

I rolled out of the bed and answered the door when Daniel knocked twice.

"Just in time," Quinn said.

Daniel handed me a bottle of wine and two glasses, setting the second bottle down on the nightstand. Apparently, his definition of a nightcap was far off from mine. "I swiped these from the kitchen. My room doesn't have any extra glasses."

"And the wine?" I asked, my brows lifting when I recognized the label as something I'd only seen locked behind glass in the liquor stores.

"What can I say?" Daniel said mildly, "people love me."

Quinn huffed a laugh. "Just open the bottle and settle in. We have some things to go over."

"Oooh. Intrigue," Daniel said, choosing a chair across from the bed.

I dug in my purse for the wine bottle opener I always kept on my keychain and focused on opening the bottle. When it was done, I poured each of us a glass. Unlike Daniel, we had several wine glasses in the small bar toward the back of the room.

"We already know Angela was a teacher's aide, but it says here she was working on a startup dealing with artificial intelligence in the classroom."

Hardy's brow furrowed. "Was she worth anything?"

Quinn's gaze skimmed down his laptop before he stilled and blew out a low whistle. "Yes. Millions."

"And she was still a teacher's aide?" I asked. Technically, I was worth millions, but I still felt an overwhelming need to work. There'd be no judgment from me.

"As far as I can tell. We should call her school tomorrow and inquire," Quinn said.

"Who knows she's worth millions?" Hardy wondered aloud.

I sipped my wine, and it was so good I immediately took a larger drink. Daniel grinned and winked at me.

"You think it's more likely whoever it was wanted her money and didn't kill her impulsively?" It was possible, but I still leaned toward the affair theory.

"We can't rule anything out," Quinn said. "Angela created a proprietary product that was the crux of the business. She owned the patent. Without her, there is no business."

"So, getting rid of her would kill the business immediately?" I shook my head. "That's awful."

"Unless she had a business partner." Quinn skimmed the file. "But I don't see one." He typed a few words and paused. "Looks like she has a hierarchy on her website, but it seems like she was the only one who knew how the tech worked."

"And then there were two," Daniel said quietly. "Two potential motives for this woman's death."

I crawled underneath the blankets again and sipped my wine. "The conversation she had with that man..." I shook my head. "It really seemed like they were having an affair, and it got out of hand."

"Is it possible they were discussing something else?" Quinn asked.

I thought about it. "If she hadn't said that thing about that man's wife and the words not long, I'd say yes, but that seemed pretty clear."

"From that, it seems like she expected him to leave her soon." Quinn scrubbed a hand over his face. "If that ring is hers, which it seems like it is, he may have placated her to buy himself more time."

"Afraid she'll tell his wife?" I asked.

"Could be that or could be he was keeping her around, waiting for her to take her company public."

Hardy shook his head. "He wouldn't be entitled to anything if they weren't married."

"That is a very good point," Quinn said. "I plan to dig a little deeper to see if she had any private investors or a life insurance policy."

I held up a hand. "Wait. If everyone here is stupid rich, why would he want her money?"

Daniel laughed. "Oh, Dakota. I adore your idealistic tendencies."

I shot him a glare.

He smiled. "You are content with the money you have. Most people are not. Money equals power. Some people gather money like little girls gather wildflowers. Why have one flower when you can have the whole bunch?"

His words made a terrible sort of sense. "So, we're just dealing with yet another terrible person?" I groaned.

Hardy chuckled and reached over to squeeze my calf. "He's already pretty terrible, but there's a difference between a crime of passion and a cold-blooded murder."

"This is my least favorite case," I muttered.

"That's because we got forced into this one," Hardy said, sympathy in his voice. "And we have yet to meet one decent person at this place."

I shrugged. "Sam seems nice."

"One then," Hardy said with amusement. "Though we can't cross her husband off the list."

I slapped a hand over my face. "Aargh! I forgot about her due to all the Kathy mess. Sam told me her husband wasn't with her during the time the murder occurred."

Quinn stopped typing. "Where was he?"

"No idea. Sam is supposed to talk to him."

"If he's guilty, he'll lie. Which one is Sam's husband?"

I had to think. Names were harder to remember than faces. "Nick, I think. He's the guy who retired young after investing."

Hardy stilled. "What did he invest in?"

My heart lurched. "Noooo," I breathed. "You don't think..."

"Did he recently retire?" Daniel asked.

"No idea. They're both young, though. Maybe early thirties?"

"What's his last name?"

"Now that I definitely don't know. I don't recall them mentioning it." In fact, only a couple of people had. "But Sam has her bakery. Maybe we can find out that way?"

"Text her and ask her the name of it," Hardy said.

I looked at him. "You don't think that's weird?"

"You're a curious person, Dakota. Everyone can see that." He gave me a winning smile that made me laugh.

"Fine," I said with a sigh as I reached for my phone.

I thought about what I wanted to say before sending her a quick message.

Hardy and I are honeymooning locally soon. We'd love to stop by your bakery if we're in the area! What's the name of it?

Guilt plucked through me as I hit send.

She responded less than a minute later.

I'd love it if you stopped by! It's called Sweet Cheeks over in Franklin.

Wonderful! I'll keep in touch and let you know what we decide.

Great!

"Sweet Cheeks in Franklin," I said to Quinn.

He nodded and typed away.

Daniel stood and reached for the wine. "What about the tech guy?"

"They're both in tech. Kristy and...David, I think." She was the one with the friendly face.

"Did they say what kind of tech?" Daniel asked.

"No, and I probably wouldn't understand it even if they did," I said with a laugh. "But, if you want to check them, too, I think their last name is Brauer."

We chatted for another half hour or so before Daniel stood and stretched. "I'm off to bed. Tomorrow might be a great time to start applying pressure to our fellow guests for their alibis." He wiggled his eyebrows. "After tonight, everyone is going to be suspicious."

"I plan to visit the injured woman tomorrow," Quinn said.

"Kathy is her name. Won't it be better if Hardy or I go?" I set my wine glass down and yawned.

"Max may not let you off the grounds. One of his employees moved all the vehicles off site."

My jaw dropped. "What?"

Quinn grinned. "Yup. Mine is still here because I'm special."

"You're special all right," I grumbled.

"Kathy is in good hands," he said. "If she remembers what happened, this case might be over tomorrow."

Daniel waved and let himself out.

"One can dream," I said.

Hardy reached over and kissed my cheek. "We'll take a nice long honeymoon to make up for this nightmare vacation."

"Somewhere warm." I pulled the covers up to my chin.

"Very warm."

"You two haven't planned your honeymoon yet?" Quinn asked us, his eyebrows almost to his hairline.

"Everything has been about the wedding," I admitted.

"What about flights? Hotels? Izzy?"

"Izzy is coming with us," Hardy said.

Quinn gaped at him. "On your honeymoon. What about..." He waved a hand at us. "Private time?"

My cheeks turned pink. "My mom and grandma are coming with us."

Quinn blinked. "Your mother-in-law is coming on your honeymoon? Good god man. You have my thoughts and prayers."

"Quinn! My mom is perfectly nice and adores both of them!"

Hardy laughed at Quinn's look of disbelief. "It's actually true. I'm very blessed to snag an Adair woman."

"But on your honeymoon, man?" Quinn let out a slow whistle. "You're much braver than me."

Hardy and I exchanged a glance. The wedding was

still a little while away, but we hadn't yet told Quinn we were planning an extended honeymoon. "How do you feel about running the office for a while?" I asked.

Quinn closed his laptop and gave me a suspicious look. "How long?"

"Maybe a month?" I winced.

He shrugged. "Meh. That's not so bad. I thought you were going to say six months. A month is nothing. Take a little longer if you like."

Hardy opened his mouth and shut it, a bemused expression crossing his handsome face. "I knew I made the right decision about you," he finally said.

"I worked alone all the time in my last position," he drawled. "As I'm sure your soon to be wife noticed."

I rolled my eyes. "Yeah. Quinn has poor social skills. It's to be expected for a law enforcement officer left to his own devices. He slowly went feral."

"Are you sure lucky is the right word, Hardy?"

"Now, now, children."

"Looks like the Brauer's are co-owners of a tech company specializing in software." He shook his head. "Can't tell what kind."

"They're not off the hook, then. Is there a way we can find out exactly what kind?" I hadn't talked to Kristy or David very much.

"Not unless we ask them directly. If they're involved, they won't give a straight answer." Quinn shut his laptop and put it on the desk close to his bed. "I'll let you know how the visit with Kathy goes tomorrow. In the meantime, an awkward goodnight to you both."

I sighed. "Some vacation this is," I grumbled. "It feels like an awkward summer camp sleepover."

"Go make out in a broom closet or something, and the dream will be complete," Quinn said.

I threw a pillow at him.

This case could not be over soon enough.

THIRTEEN

Daniel was right. Everyone was on edge this morning. I poured myself a cup of coffee from the carafe, my shoulders itching with the weight of a dozen stares. Hardy stood close by, fixing himself a small plate of fruit.

Quinn was already on his way to the hospital, and we left Poppy snuggled up in her bed when we left. Daniel hadn't come down yet, but he rarely rose early.

Everyone was here this morning, dressed to the nines, but almost everyone wore serious expressions even as their eyes darted between everyone inside the dining room.

Even Max had deigned to show up, his stare lingering on me for a moment too long. His eyes were unreadable, but even an idiot could tell how displeased he was by me.

No one was pleased when a murder dropped into their lap, but Max was a man with secrets to hide, and I suspected as each day passed, we moved closer and closer to uncovering them.

When the clock hit the top of the hour, Max picked up a champagne flute and tapped it a few times.

Hardy and I made our way to our seats, settling quietly while Max began to speak.

"I'm sure last night was difficult for everyone. Rest assured, I contacted the hospital earlier this morning and Kathy is expected to make a full recovery."

Polite clapping sounded all around, and I barely suppressed my cringe.

"Yes, my head gardener is made of sturdy stock. She'll be back with more beautiful flower displays within weeks."

Ah yes. The flower displays. That's what's important here.

"While the police investigate what happened to her, I must ask you to refrain from rampant speculation. Kathy has been known to trip and fall in that greenhouse, though this is the first time she's suffered such a serious injury."

"My understanding is the wound is at the back of her head," I chimed in. "That would be very difficult to achieve in a fall."

Max's left eye twitched. "As I said, we must leave the speculation up to the police. Right now, it's too soon to know exactly what happened. We must keep Kathy in our prayers."

It took everything I had not to roll my eyes. "What if it wasn't an accident?" I pressed. "Should we be taking extra precautions in and around the mansion?"

A few of the couples shifted uncomfortably.

Hardy laid a hand on my knee and squeezed gently,

warning me to lay off. I reached down and squeezed back, just a hair harder.

"Steinhoffer Mansion has state-of-the-art security, but to answer your *direct* question, I've reached out to a private security company this morning and asked for more assistance in upping my current security recalls. You are as safe here at Steinhoffer as you would be in your own homes."

I smiled, a thing of sharp edges. "I've never had a murder in my home, so I may have a little trouble taking your word for it."

Max's eyes sparked with anger. "We have one more day until the rare manuscript arrives, but this evening Daniel Jensen has gracefully accepted my invitation to do a reading of his as of yet unpublished book, *The Raven's Dark Call.*"

Daniel hadn't mentioned this book to me. Not that we hung out as much as we did, so I guess he had no reason to, but I felt a pang at knowing our friendship wasn't what it used to be. We were still close, yes, but I was missing out on a lot of his achievements. But...Hardy sat beside me, and this was part of moving on with him. I couldn't regret it because it brought me to him.

"That's wonderful news," Mary exclaimed. "I don't read much genre fiction, but I took the liberty of looking him up, and it looks like his books have a strong literary slant."

Not true, but I held my tongue. If she wanted to market his books, I wouldn't stop her. Plus, I always wondered if people truly meant it when they said they didn't enjoy genre fiction. How could you not enjoy thrilling adventure and heart pounding suspense? Or cozy romance or...magic and dragons? Not all of those things were everyone's cup of tea, but where I liked magic, someone else liked mayhem and murder.

And since genre made up most of television and fiction, I had to think that if they didn't like it, then maybe they just hadn't found the right thing for them yet.

"He's a wonderful author," I said to everyone at the table. "I'm sure whatever he's working on next will be fabulous."

And just like that, the tension broke. Servers came through a door holding covered silver trays, and once again we were eating. Maybe we'd skip lunch today just to have more time to explore.

We still hadn't come up with a plan to break into everyone's rooms yet, but if we skipped lunch, we could hit two or three rooms at least.

But what if Max had cameras? I sat up straighter. Did Max have cameras? If so, had he shown those to the police?

Daniel entered the room right as the first course was served, pulling out the chair I'd saved for him. I pushed my still hot cup of coffee toward him.

"God bless you, Dakota Adair," he murmured under his breath. "You are a saint among women."

I snorted. "I didn't want to speak to you until you had your caffeine. Getting my head bitten off at seven in the morning is never fun."

His teeth flashed in a slight grin as he picked the mug up and sipped, his eyes fluttering shut as the first taste hit his tongue. "Nectar of the gods," he croaked.

"Up late?" I asked.

"The writer's bane," he agreed. "I get an idea of a scene in my head and no matter where or when it is, I must get it down on paper or on a document. It must have been two a.m. before I crawled into bed."

I winced. "I'm surprised you're here."

He shrugged. "The faster we solve this case, the faster we can get home."

"I'm sure you can leave any time," I said quietly. "You've known Max for a while. Surely he wouldn't keep you here?"

The edges of his eyes crinkled. "I don't think he would, but I won't leave you here. Not with a second victim."

"Max said Kathy will be okay." I leaned back as the server placed the first course in front of me and lowered my voice. "But he's trying to pass it off as an accident."

"Liability," Daniel said quietly.

"Yeah, and they ate it up like candy."

He rolled his eyes. "No one wants to live in fear. It's always easier to ignore the bad things in the world than face them. Especially for people who've grown up privileged."

"So, if nothing bad has ever happened to them, it won't ever happen?"

He chuckled. "Pretty much. It's a little delusional, but it works for them and helps them sleep at night."

"I wish I could be that delusional," I grumbled.

Hardy gently elbowed me and leaned to whisper in my ear. "You two are starting to attract attention."

Daniel winked at me. "Don't make them too jealous, darling. They're already positively green with envy at you sandwiched between two strapping men."

"You're incorrigible," I huffed.

Breakfast was a somewhat somber affair, at least when compared with yesterday. When it was over, no one milled about too much, instead filing out to explore or bunch up into social cliques. Hardy, Daniel, and I escaped back to our room. Quinn was still gone, and Poppy waited at the door for us, loudly protesting our absence.

"You've already eaten, sassy pants," I chided.

Poppy jumped onto my bed, her tail swishing, and eyed me as if to say, "so what." I reached into the night-stand drawer, one of the few places safe from Poppy's curiosity because it was so heavy and pulled out a bag of snacks for her.

She took one from me and crunched, eyeing us as we shrugged off our shoes.

"What if we snuck out of here?" I pondered as I sank into one of the chairs and closed my eyes. "Just packed it all up and left?"

Hardy gave me a long look. "You'd be able to live with yourself?"

I cracked an eye open. "Could you?"

"I have an entire file drawer dedicated to the cases I

couldn't solve." He sighed. "One gets used to it after a while."

Daniel raised his hands. "Don't look at me. Every crime I've been involved in is solved."

"Because they're fictional," I said, exasperated.

He laughed. "And because the real-life ones had an ace sleuth involved."

Hardy snorted. "Quit flirting with my wife."

My heart skipped a beat.

"Not quite," Daniel said. "Your almost wife. I still have..." he held up his phone and peered at the screen, "three weeks and two days to win her over."

"Can we get back to discussing whether we can blow this joint and pretend we never came here?" I said, rubbing the space between my brows. A headache was creeping up on me, a result of stress, little sleep, and homesickness. Poppy jumped into my lap and bapped me on the nose. "I guess the answer is no?"

Poppy bapped me more gently the second time. I scratched between her ears. "I know. I'd never leave, especially since no one else seems to be helping this poor girl."

The sound of a key entering the lock announced Quinn's presence. He loosened his tie as soon as he stepped in, tugging it off to throw on top of his bed. "Ugh," he said by way of greeting. "The weather's getting bad out there."

I frowned as I realized I hadn't checked the weather report in days. "If we got involved in all this and tomorrow's event gets canceled due to weather, I'm going to scream."

Quinn kicked off his shoes and flopped onto his bed. "Worse than that is us getting snowed in."

I looked at him in horror. "Bite your tongue, sir."

He blew out a breath and stared up at the ceiling. "Did you figure out how we're going to hit all the rooms?"

"Wait for lunchtime, I suppose. Though it would be suspicious if all of us were gone." We'd have to split up and send at least one person to the dining room. "I vote Daniel eats lunch and keeps everyone charmed with his ridiculous stories."

Daniel's eyes narrowed. "I think by ridiculous you actually mean charming."

"Sure," I said with a slow nod. "My mistake."

He harrumphed and crossed his arms. "I will absolutely volunteer to have a three-course lunch and talk to rich people."

Hardy's eyes twinkled with amusement. "Quinn and I will go. Dakota, try to rein him in at least a little."

"I make no promises."

Daniel stretched. "What do we do if someone tries to leave?"

"Don't let them," Quinn advised. "And if you still can't stop them. Text us both and tell us who it is so we can get out in time."

"And if someone skips do the same?" I inquired.

"We need to know who's out of their rooms so we don't accidentally run into someone. That would bring up a lot of questions we don't have the answers for," Quinn said.

"Got it," I said. "How's Kathy?"

"Recovering." Quinn reached an arm out for his laptop. "She was hit from behind but doesn't know with what. One hit only."

"Does she suspect why?" Hardy asked.

"She heard someone or something in the greenhouse when she was doing her final walk-through to bring the flowers in. When she went to investigate, someone came up behind her and hit her."

"She didn't see a thing then," Hardy said, his voice full of frustration.

"Not exactly. She was able to turn and see the person running out."

Hardy's attention sharpened. "Man? Woman?"

"Male. Kathy said he was tall, but she was lying on the floor so her perception may be altered."

"Did she catch any details?" I asked. "Hair color? Clothing?"

Quinn sat up. "Too dark for an exact hair color, but she knew it wasn't blond. He wore a camel-colored jacket."

Daniel was shaking his head. "What on earth could they have been looking for in a greenhouse?"

Considering we'd talk to Kathy on the night she was injured, I wasn't sure they were looking for anything at all. "Maybe they were waiting on her."

Daniel crossed an ankle over his knee. "You think he was trying to keep her from talking again?"

"Or punishing her," I agreed. "For talking to us in the first place."

"What I don't understand," Quinn said, "is why he wouldn't finish her off?"

"I can answer that," Hardy interjected. "He probably heard Dakota and Samantha talking when they got close to the greenhouse. It spooked him and he ran away."

My stomach squeezed. "Do you think she's still in danger?"

"There are two officers on the door. As long as there are no security lapses, Kathy should be okay."

"Security lapses in the form of a bribe?" Daniel drawled. "Money seems to do a lot of the talking around here."

Quinn let out a long-suffering sigh. "I hate this place." He pulled out his cell phone. "Let me call Kevin and ensure he has his best guys on her."

"Thank you," I said quietly. "Kathy didn't do anything wrong."

"That doesn't seem to matter these days," Daniel said. He rose and headed toward the door. "My words await me, and I must attend to them." He gave a silly little bow. "Dakota, I'll pick you up at twelve for our lunch date. Wear something spectacular."

I waved him away as he exited the room.

"That guy is insufferable sometimes," Quinn said. "And he obviously has a massive crush on you."

"Who, Hardy?" I asked innocently.

Hardy gave me an exasperated look.

BOOK CLUB BAIT & SWITCH   127

"You know who," Quinn growled. "You're still friends with him?"

I took a deep breath. "Daniel has been nothing but kind to me, Quinn. He's a friend and nothing more. The only boundaries he pushes are verbal, and it's only to needle Hardy."

"I don't like it," Quinn growled.

"Daniel and I know where the other stands," Hardy said. "Though I appreciate your support."

I glanced between them, curious. After the first case, Hardy and Quinn had bonded. They had a lot in common and seemed to get along like two peas in a pod. This is the first time Quinn ever had a cross word to say about Daniel, and it both annoyed me and warmed me.

He was right, though, and I hated Quinn being right about anything. Daniel should respect my boundaries, and it wasn't right of me to keep brushing his words off if they were needling Hardy.

I'd talk to Daniel at lunch time.

"I'll keep an eye out for a blazer or suit jacket with a missing button while we're in the dining room," I said after an awkward pause.

"And we'll look for empty ring boxes and the same thing," Quinn said. "Mind letting me take another look at that ring?"

I got up to dig it out and hand it to him. He held it up to the light. "There's a maker's mark inside, but I can't see it."

"Maybe take a picture and zoom in?" Hardy suggested.

Quinn did, but even when he enlarged the picture, he shook his head. "No idea. Probably some luxury brand us peons don't know about."

"Hold it up?" I suggested as I rose to take a closer look.

The mark looked like an odd trident with a line through the middle. "Send me the picture. I'm in a jewelry identification thread. I bet someone there can help me out."

"Under a fake name?" Hardy inquired.

"Millenial Jewelry Hoarder."

My fiancé burst out laughing. "Every time I think I know all there is to know about you, I find out something even stranger."

I rubbed my hands together. "Just you wait," I said slyly. "I'm a woman of mystery."

My phone buzzed.

"Just sent it. Crop out as much of the ring as you can. We don't want anyone to stumble on the thread and figure out we're on to them."

I gave him a quelling look. "This is not my first rodeo."

Quinn held his hands up. "Sorry, Miss PI. I always err on the safe versus sorry side."

I logged on to the ID site and made a post. Sometimes when I went thrifting, I'd pick up a piece of jewelry I needed help placing. Sometimes it was the time period, and sometimes there'd be a mark I didn't recognize. There wasn't a single time someone didn't have the answer, so I knew we'd have an answer within a few hours at most.

"There," I said. "I'll let you know what they say. Why do you think it will help?"

"I have a few buddies who can get the records for me if we end up needing them."

"But don't you need the purchase date?" Wherever this was probably sold the same ring every day. It might be difficult pinning down the exact buyer if we didn't have a date.

"If this place is as exclusive as the rest of the places these people frequent, it may be much easier than you think to nail down the buyer."

Hardy rose and grabbed his jacket. "Want to take a walk?" he asked.

I blinked. "In a winter storm?"

He grinned, those sapphire eyes twinkling. "It's a good time to do another check of the greenhouse. The light is better, and it's not too far of a walk. No one else will be out, so we don't have to worry about interruptions."

I grumbled about it but put on a few more layers, gloves, a wool scarf and a hat. "You coming?" I asked Quinn.

"Not a chance in the world," he said, wiggling his fingers at us in a mocking wave.

"You're lucky we need you to man the shop," I muttered.

Quinn flashed a grin. "Yes, yes I am."

FOURTEEN

My teeth started chattering less than a minute into the walk. "Y-y-you o-o-owe me," I said.

Hardy slung an arm around me. "All the hot chocolate you can stand tonight."

"W-w-ith Irish c-c-cream and w-w-hipped cream?"

He winced. "You run a hard bargain. I'll have to raid the kitchen."

"Y-you b-better."

The greenhouse loomed above us, gray and forbidding in the frigid weather. Suddenly, the place held a sinister air. Hardy pushed the door open with a grunt and motioned me in.

I hurried inside, snow blasting against our backs as Hardy struggled with the door. He finally got it shut with a loud thump, sealing us into an eerie silence. A bulb on a thin wire swung wildly overhead, sending flashes of light around the place, casting strange shadows as it swayed.

Even with the winter weather, the place smelled of damp earth and loam. I inhaled, itching to dig my fingers into fresh dirt, but Kathy would scream bloody murder if anything was out of place when she returned. Hardy blew into his hands and stomped his feet.

All I did was stand there with chattering teeth, glaring at my fiancé for making me come out in the snow.

He chuckled and drew me in for a hug. "Cranky pants."

"It's freezing out there and we were in a perfectly warm bedroom," I grumbled. But I wasn't mad at him. Just the situation. I melted into his warmth for a moment before pulling away. "I love greenhouses. No matter how bad the weather is outside, they always feel cozy." It wasn't so warm I could start stripping layers, but it wasn't the bone-chilling cold from outside.

"When we start seriously looking for a new place, we can build one."

I gaped at him. "Oh my gosh, we *could* do that, couldn't we?"

He grinned and pressed a cold kiss to my forehead. "We can do anything you want."

"And you," I added, lest he think the money I had wouldn't be his when we got married.

"We can talk about that later. In the meantime, let's dig around and see if we find anything out of place."

"And then get back inside and thaw in front of a fireplace."

"Absolutely. You stay in the front, and I'll dig around in the back. Meet in ten?"

"You got it."

Hardy ventured toward the back, and I turned in a circle, looking for anything out of place.

Kathy might be crabby, but she was organized. Everything was neatly labeled, the contents documented in a spidery cursive. She had multiple types of dirt, numerous soil additives, and more seeds than I'd ever seen before. I picked through drawers and bags, searched through shelves and paid special attention to the floor.

"Hardy?"

"Hmm?"

"Did they find the weapon?"

"Not that I'm aware of. Why?"

"Just asking." If the perp dropped it, maybe they could get fingerprints off it. But...it was winter, and most people wore gloves all the time now, especially if they were outside. Worth a shot, though. You never knew when a criminal might make a dumb mistake.

I searched through the two aisles on either side, my gaze eventually snagging on a cylindrical piece of wood lying on its side, partially concealed by one of the potting tables. It had either rolled or been shoved against the table's feet.

My heartbeat picked up as I crouched and turned on my cell flashlight to get a closer look. A spot of red gleamed on the edge.

"Hardy, I think I found something."

"I did, too." I glanced up to see Hardy looming over me. He held something white in his hand.

"No way," I mused. "Another button?"

"Either this guy got a bum jacket, or both victims tore one off as they struggled." He tucked it into his pocket. "We need to find who these belong to."

I motioned for him to crouch beside me. "Think this is something?"

Hardy's jaw tightened when he saw what I was looking at. "Good find." He reached for it carefully, picking it up as much as he could before sliding the rest out. "It's not a bat." Hardy stood and hefted it. "Solid oak. Kathy is lucky she's alive."

"What is it?" I asked as I readjusted my scarf.

"No idea. Maybe something to break up potting soil?"

I'd never seen its like before. "Let's let the police figure it out."

"I'll have Quinn run it in. No need to let Max see we found something."

"I don't like that guy," I admitted. "Something about him gives me the creeps."

"Many things about him give me the creeps. He's the worst kind of rich person—the kind who uses money to control rather than empower."

I blinked at him. "That's...a great way to describe him."

"I dealt with many people like him over the years. Quinn's bound to have dealt with even more."

I looped my arm through his. "I'm sorry."

"Not your fault. All those bad experiences led me right to you."

"Aww," I murmured. "Sweet talker."

We walked out together arm in arm, the potential murder weapon swinging by his other side.

QUINN'S JAW dropped when he saw what Hardy carried. "You definitely spooked him last night, Dakota."

"She was very lucky he decided to cut and run," Hardy said, a grim twist to his mouth.

"Having Sam there helped."

We still had a couple of hours until lunch. I skimmed over the schedule. "There's a coffee and tea mixer downstairs. I think I'm going to attend and see what I can find out."

"I'll leave you to it," Hardy said. "Quinn and I need to come up with a game plan for lunch time."

I grabbed a fresh sweater and a pair of Ponte pants and headed into the restroom to change. Poppy was nowhere to be found. I hoped she was still in the house. She liked snow more than the average cat, but I didn't want her to get caught outside with no way to get back in. The temperatures outside were downright dangerous today.

Once I'd reapplied some lip gloss and blush and slipped on some ballet flats and a thin cardigan, I was ready to go. Hardy's eyes lit up when he saw me. "You look good," he murmured, bringing me in for a hug.

Quinn's disgusted snort made me laugh. "The next

time you two get caught up in some harebrained scheme, I am not sharing a room with you. I'm going to expense it. As it is, I feel like I should be paid triple time after being exposed to all this mushy nonsense."

"Your contract says all overtime must be approved in advance," Hardy murmured against my hair, his voice amused.

"Yeah well, I demand a re-read," Quinn said.

I gently nudged Hardy. "Are you going to ask?" I whispered.

"Ask what?" Quinn demanded.

Sometimes I thought the guy had paranormal hearing abilities. It felt like he could hear a pin drop in the woods when the wind was blowing.

Hardy let me go and turned to face Quinn, whose eyebrows lifted before his eyes narrowed. "Do I need to be concerned about this?"

"Only if you hate love," Hardy said.

I smacked his arm. "Be nice," I chided.

He rolled his eyes. "Quinn, I was wondering if you're free on December 14th."

Quinn frowned. "I certainly hope so. You invited me to your wedding after all."

"Yes, but are you free the entire day?"

Quinn tilted his head in curiosity. "Yeeeeessss," he said slowly, drawing out the word. "Why?"

"I was wondering if you'd be my best man?"

Silence fell in the room. Quinn's eyes widened before a suspicious sheen appeared in them. I looked down at my feet and headed over to the chair where I quietly sat down to wait.

"First of all," Quinn croaked. "You two are the worst wedding planners I've ever met."

Hardy cracked a laugh. "Yes, well, if it weren't for our families, we would have eloped by now. All these details are a little overwhelming, and I kept forgetting to ask because I knew you'd be there. But apparently there are duties a best man has to attend to and…"

Quinn walked the few steps over to Hardy and brought him into a crushing embrace, slapping him on the back twice before stepping back to compose himself.

"I guess that's a yes?" Hardy said after a long pause.

"Yes," Quinn said. "I'd be honored to act as your best man."

The two men stared at each other, and Hardy nodded, once. "Then I guess that settles it."

A smile pulled at my lips. Men. It really was just that easy for them sometimes.

THE COFFEE and tea get together was more crowded than I expected. I spotted Sam first and made a beeline for her, waving as I walked into the room.

She held a cup of steaming coffee and a pastry, though I noticed she'd only taken a single bite out of it.

"Is it hard eating other people's dessert when you're a baker?" I asked when I came up beside her.

She blinked, then glanced down at her plate, blushing

when she realized she'd been caught. "Oh. Yes." She sighed. "I try so hard, but I notice all the things I would have done differently. More butter or maybe less butter. Less mixing time, more rising time." Sam rolled her eyes. "It's a sickness I can't seem to cure."

"I judge people who dog-ear their books," I admitted in a hushed voice.

Sam snorted. "Yes, but you can do that quietly. I have to do the walk of shame back to the tray and put my uneaten pastry on it and hope no one sees me."

"Life is too short to eat bad pastry."

We smiled at each other and watched as two other couples walked in, smiling and nodding as they made their way over to a small circular area filled with four chairs and a small table.

"Want to sit down?" I asked.

"I'd love to, but I need a place that has room for Nick. He should be here in about twenty minutes."

"Oh, wonderful. I'm sure we can find something."

I led Sam through the room and found a spot with a small table over toward the right corner. Mary and Heath James stood close by. She gave us a cool nod as we settled in and returned her attention to her husband and the couple they spoke with—the author and his editor wife. Mike and...

"Sarah," Sam whispered. "Mike and Sarah, I think."

I snapped my fingers. "That's it. I remembered his name, but I couldn't remember hers."

"She's quiet. Mike is the more talkative of the two."

It was true. He carried most of the conversation, though he had a softer than normal pitch and a soothing tone to his voice that would serve him well if he ever decided to narrate meditation videos.

I leaned in toward Sarah. "Did you ask Nick about his whereabouts?" I murmured.

Sarah suddenly found her coffee cup very interesting. "I did. He said he needed to get out of the room and wanted to clear his head."

That didn't sound good.

"Did anyone see him?"

"He said he had a drink with Max." She rolled her eyes. "And it's not like I can go right up to Max and ask him."

"Well, you could, couldn't you?"

She laughed uncomfortably. "Not all of us are as brave as you."

I blinked in surprise. "Brave?"

"Of course. Very few people actually speak their mind, Dakota. They're always so concerned with how everyone sees them, but you don't seem to care about that."

At my befuddled look, she smiled. "It's not a bad trait. I wish I could say what I was thinking." She sighed. "Or what is necessary."

I guess I never thought about it that way. "It's probably my mother's fault." My lips twisted. "Maybe even my grandmother's. Or maybe it's just an Adair trait. There aren't many in my family who don't say what they're thinking." I chuckled to myself. "You always know where you stand with an Adair."

"And that's refreshing because you know how women are." She sat back in her seat and tilted her chin to the ceiling. "We all want people to like us." Sam made a disgusting noise. "As if that was the most important thing in our lives. Being liked."

I empathized with her, though I was less inclined to care much about it. Everyone wanted to be liked in some capacity, but I always thought it was more important to share your life with people who loved you. It's far easier to be liked if you had a tribe. That wasn't to say I went out of my way to be disliked. It was always easier to be myself. Whether someone liked that or disliked it wasn't really any of my business.

"I think life becomes a lot easier when you stop caring about what everyone else feels and focus on what you feel."

She glanced at me.

"Do you want people who you don't like to like you?"

Sam blinked. "Uh. Well, I suppose I do, I guess."

"Why?"

A silence fell between us. "I don't rightly know," she said after a moment, before she laughed and took a sip of her coffee.

My mother's words came back to me, and I wondered if they'd help Sam. "Mom always told me it wasn't any of my business what someone else thought about me. I couldn't control it, so why should I waste the time worrying about it?"

Sam's lips curved into a smile. "Your mother sounds like a wise woman."

"I certainly didn't think so when I was a teenager, and she was spouting off nuggets like that."

We shared a look of commiseration. Almost every teenage daughter gave their mothers a run for their money during the years of fourteen to seventeen, sometimes even longer.

"But I'm happy to admit I was wrong. We could all stand to listen to our mothers a little more."

"Isn't that the truth?" she murmured. "Anyhow, Nick won't admit where he was. He swears he shared a drink with Max, but there's no way for me to know." Her eyes flashed, and she sat up a little straighter. "Speaking of, he's here. Mind keeping this between us?"

I nodded. "Of course." Nick greeted his wife with a kiss on her cheek and nodded to me before he took the seat next to her.

"Dakota," I said.

"Ah yes. The bookstore owner, correct?"

"That's me."

Nick was handsome in a familiar way. Strong jaw, full lips, dark, floppy hair, and a too white, too-straight smile. He'd fit right in if he lived in California. Sam, on the other hand, was shorter, curvier, and had a pretty heart-shaped face surrounded by wild, curly hair.

I rose. "I'm going to grab a drink. I'll be right back."

The coffee carafe was on the other side of the room, allowing me time to study everyone as they pretended they weren't doing the same thing.

I didn't really want anything to drink, but I spotted Kristy and David Brauer walking in, and I wanted the opportunity to chat with them. The coffee mugs the staff set out were barely eight ounces, which didn't actually qualify to be an official cup of coffee, but I grabbed one anyway and smiled as I poured myself one.

"Hi! Crazy weather we're having out there."

Kristy looked the picture of understated elegance. She wore a black-and-white striped t-shirt, an emerald green cardigan, navy Ponte pants similar to my own, and a pair of pointed toe flats with bows on their tops. Her husband looked like he'd just walked off a yacht. He wore a navy blazer and crisp tan slacks with shiny brown loafers.

"We have a fireplace in our room, thankfully. There's nothing better than curling up with a good book in front of that thing."

"I don't think I'd ever leave my room if we had one in ours." I shook my head. "We do have an amazing window with a chaise lounge. But since it's so cold, I find myself hard pressed to enjoy sitting in front of a frigid window without three extra layers on!"

Kristy smiled, and for once in this awful vacation, it reached her eyes. "So true. 40% of my luggage is cardigans." She turned to her husband. "Honey, do you remember Dakota? She's the one who owns that bookstore."

David nodded. "Of course. It's a pleasure to chat with you."

"Same."

"You were the one to discover Kathy, weren't you?" David said.

What a strange and abrupt, interesting change of subject. "I was. Me and Sam, actually."

"What happened?"

Kristy laid a hand on her husband's arm. "David—"

"If there's someone out there hurting people, we should know all the facts," he protested.

Or fish for information to see if we're on to him, I thought.

"I can't tell you much, other than I heard she's going to be okay."

A flash of something appeared over his face. Relief? Regret?

"Did you see what happened to her?" Kristy asked.

"No. We arrived right after it happened."

"Poor thing." Kristy clucked her tongue. "I hope she's okay."

"What about that other woman?" David blurted. "Know what happened to her?"

No one knew I semi-witnessed the crime. I shook my head. "Nothing other than what I heard. Just that she was attacked in Max's library."

Kristy leaned a little closer. "David heard she was stabbed."

My eyebrows hitched up. "Oh really? That's terrible.

Have the police come round to speak to anyone about what happened?"

"I think they talked to Mary and James, but we haven't seen them. What about you?"

"Hardy and I spoke to them not long ago." I eyed David. "So she was stabbed? That's terrible. Did they find the murder weapon?"

David shrugged. "No idea."

"I didn't hear much about the attack, but I did hear she was working on something that made her extremely wealthy."

Kristy's expression turned curious. "I heard she was some kind of teacher. Was it something to do with her job?"

"Strangely enough, I heard it had something to do with tech. A type of software, I think?"

Kristy nudged David. "What a shame! We work with a lot of software. I wonder if it's something we might have been interested in."

"Too late now," David murmured.

I barely held in my wince. Either this guy was just that clueless or he had something to do with her death.

"David!" Kristy reprimanded. "I'm so sorry. My husband wasn't born with a filter."

He snickered. "Neither one of us knew the woman, so it's not like we had any emotional connection to her."

"She was someone's daughter, David," Kristy said quietly, a tremor in her voice. Though she looked at her feet when she said it. Guilt? Or genuine empathy?

He waved a hand at her. "I'm aware. Please, darling, I'm not a complete monster."

I wasn't so sure about that but stuck around because I saw an opportunity to get more info. "What kind of software does your company sell?"

David's lips thinned, but Kristy spoke first. "We develop in all kinds of areas. Our company holds several patents, isn't that right, David?"

He nodded, the edges of his eyes tightening. David did not like this subject, so naturally, I pressed. "That's so cool. Are you getting into anything with artificial intelligence?"

Kristy lit up. "Yes!"

David cleared his throat.

"I obviously can't say much about it right now, but we have big plans to move into the AI space and expand our business."

"That's awesome! I don't know much about AI, but some of those deep fakes are concerning."

She waved a hand. "Oh, it's nothing like that. We're hoping to go into the—"

David took Kristy by the elbow. "I'm so sorry. I forgot we have a meeting here in ten minutes upstairs." He rolled his eyes. "An investor call."

Kristy blinked. "What—"

"Don't you remember, honey?" He smiled apologetically. "I hope we get to catch up later," he said as he pulled his wife away.

That guy might not be guilty of murder, but he was definitely guilty of something.

FIFTEEN

Quinn and Hardy had changed into casual clothes. Nothing too obvious like ski masks and all black clothing, but they were both in dark clothing and wearing scarves, something they could easily loosen and cover their faces with if need be.

Daniel sat in our recliner, staring at both with a bemused expression. "This feels like one of those buddy comedies where one is responsible, and the other is a rebel with a death wish, but in this instant, I can't tell who is who."

"They're both responsible," I said, tossing my purse onto the table by the door. I kicked off my flats with a groan and flopped onto the bed. "I wish we had a fireplace."

Daniel laughed. "I have one."

I sighed and tossed one of the throw pillows at him. "Switch rooms with us," I begged.

"Not on your life. Three's a crowd, Dakota."

Hardy sat beside me. "Find out anything interesting?"

I sat up. "David Brauer is kind of a creep. I don't know if he's guilty, but he was awfully curious about Kathy and Angela. When I asked about their company, Kristy started talking about some of the software they're developing, and he pulled her away. Quickly."

"It doesn't mean he's guilty," Quinn said, "but it's something we should keep an eye out for. Tech folks are notoriously private about their upcoming projects. His questions about Kathy and Angela might be due to nosiness, but I agree about keeping a closer eye on him."

"I think you should keep your distance for now," Hardy added.

Hardy and I both knew how well I did that, but I nodded anyway. By the time I'd made it back to Sam, they'd left the event, so I never had the chance to probe about Nick's whereabouts.

I mentioned as much to everyone.

"Hopefully in the next hour, we'll have concrete proof about who's responsible for this," Quinn said.

"What about Max?" I asked.

"He was in the study and left you there, didn't he?" Hardy asked.

"He did." I saw him walk out the same door we used.

"Max seems intelligent. It would be the height of foolishness for him to know you're in there and do something like that."

"But what if he did something else?" I wondered aloud.

BOOK CLUB BAIT & SWITCH 147

Curiosity crept over Daniel's face. "Like what?"

I threw an arm over my face and sighed. "I dunno. He's a terrible person, so surely he's guilty of something."

Everyone laughed. "We can't arrest terrible people," Quinn chided. "Twenty percent of the population might be in jail if we could."

"Maybe we should try his rooms too." Something about him bothered me. I couldn't put my finger on it. Yes, he was a terrible person, but was he a murderer? Hardy was right. It would be insanely stupid for him to commit a murder knowing I was there. But what if he didn't know? I was in there for a while, losing myself in a book. Did he think I was long gone? Had he forgotten I was there?

I rubbed my temples.

"It's a lot riskier to do that to Max than it is to the others," Quinn said, but there was a twinkle of adventure in his eyes.

"I think it's far easier for me to explain myself if I got caught there than any of you," Daniel interjected. "I could always say I was interested in his writing craft books or something of the sort. Whereas if he caught you, he'd know you were snooping."

"But you're with us," I said. "Aren't you already under suspicion?"

Daniel waved a dismissive hand. "Not at all. I'm a writer. I'm supposed to hang out with shady people."

"Shady!" I shot him a heated glare. "The only shady people in this place are the author and his friends." Emphasizing the last word, I also used finger quotes. I'd bet my left kidney no one here was actually friends, not in the same definition normal people used.

He grinned. "So touchy, Dakota. You know I don't think any of you are shady, but Max does."

"He doesn't think so either," Hardy said. "But he is afraid of us and what we might uncover."

"I still think we shouldn't be so quick to let him off the hook." My stomach churned. I had far too much coffee today and not enough water. "If he shows up for lunch, I'll let you know."

"No guarantees," Hardy said.

My email pinged. A quick glance revealed someone from the thread had answered my question about the maker's mark on that ring.

"Ever heard of Trident Stones?" I asked the room. "That's where the ring was made."

Everyone had blank stares. I did an online search. "Looks like they're in New York. They specialize in diamond and precious stone jewelry." A quick scan made me gasp. "A ring that looks suspiciously like the one we found runs about twenty grand."

Quinn whistled. "Chump change here, though. I bet someone has a pair of pants that cost half that."

"Can you imagine?" I murmured. "Money like that could be someone's entire yearly earnings. That ring was just discarded."

"I wonder if anyone asked about it," Daniel said.

"That's a good point. Should I mention I found a ring

and see what happens?" If I brought it up at lunch, I'd be able to spot if anyone reacted.

"Couldn't hurt," Hardy said, "but don't tell them what kind it is. Make them identify it."

"Daniel, still coming to lunch?" I asked.

"Absolutely. I'm invested now." He kicked back his chair. "Where's that cat of yours?"

I hadn't seen her when I came in, and she usually didn't hide when it was just us. "She must have snuck out."

"Knowing that cat, she'll drag the murderer back here by the collar," Quinn muttered.

"One can hope." I scrolled through my email making sure there was nothing else I needed to take care of before tucking my phone back into my purse. "I'd keep Poppy in a permanent supply of her favorite treats if she got us out of here sooner."

"Don't let her hear you say that," Hardy said. "She'll never leave you alone."

True. Poppy loved her treats. "Either way, I'm sure she'll be fine roaming the mansion."

We chatted for a little while longer until it was time to separate. I kissed Hardy goodbye and slipped out of the room with Daniel.

Silence fell between us until we reached the top of the stairs.

"Daniel? Can we chat for a moment?"

"Always," he said, offering me his elbow as we descended the stairs.

I curled my fingers around his arm. "Please stop antagonizing Hardy."

Daniel stilled. "What?"

I tried to take another step, but he held me still. "Is that what you think I'm doing?" A flicker of hurt crossed his face.

"Isn't it?"

Daniel blinked. "No. Not at all. Men normally rib each other, Dakota. Our history is stranger than most, and I've made no secret I lost you." He smiled sadly. "While I've made my peace with it, I have to admit it still rankles me."

"For what it's worth, I'm sorry."

"There's no need to apologize. Our hearts rarely follow where our minds want it to go." We continued back down the steps.

"I don't want Hardy to ever doubt how I feel about him," I said quietly. "And I feel like it's disrespectful when you tease him about me."

Daniel stopped again and gave me a long look before he nodded once, sharply. "You're right. I'm sorry, Dakota. It will not happen again."

My throat tightened. "Are you angry?"

His nostrils flared. "At you? No. At myself, absolutely. I had no idea my teasing affected you so much."

"I'm more concerned about Hardy. I know you and I are in a good spot, but Hardy is showing a lot of trust letting us hang out. I want you in my life, Daniel, but we have to set some boundaries."

He bowed his head and exhaled, opening his arms. I stepped into the circle of his embrace, and he hugged me tightly before stepping back. "Hardy," he said, his voice thick, "is an extremely lucky man."

"I'm even luckier." Blinking away tears, I smiled. "Now. Are we ready to go catch a murderer?"

"Absolutely." He held his arm out again. "Shall we, milady?'

I dipped my head in a nod. "Yes, we shall."

SIXTEEN

The lunch bell rang at the top of the hour. Everyone, including Max, showed up. I pulled my phone out and texted, keeping it in my lap.

Everyone is here, including Max.

Got it. Be careful.

I tucked my phone in my cardigan pocket and focused on the lunch, even as my heart pounded wildly in my chest.

"Relax," Daniel whispered in my ear.

Mary James' gaze lingered on us. "Don't you two look cozy?"

Daniel stiffened.

"Hardy couldn't make it?" she asked.

I bit down the snappish retort on the tip of my tongue. "He has some work to catch up on and sent Daniel as my bodyguard."

"Must be nice to have two handsome, strapping men around all the time." Her eyes glittered.

What brought this on? I shrugged. "Daniel is one of our closest friends. He's part of the family."

Not that I owed her any explanation whatsoever, but I couldn't risk alienating anyone here if I wanted answers.

"Oh! Before I forget," I continued, "I found a gorgeous ring in Max's library. Is anyone missing any jewelry?"

No one had an overt reaction, but a few people looked back and forth as if they were looking for the same reaction I was.

"What does it look like?" Brian asked. He was the one from Kentucky, but he and his partner kept to themselves most of the time. While they showed up for meals, they hadn't clicked with anyone else.

"I thought you might tell me," I said and smiled sweetly.

He frowned but didn't push. His wife, Wendy, spoke up. "I can't find a Claddagh ring I bought. Was that it?"

I wondered if she was fishing, but I answered her anyway. "No, sorry. It wasn't a Claddagh."

"Darn," she said quietly. "I wonder where I left it."

I smiled politely. "I hope you find it. If anyone else is missing any jewelry, please come and talk to me. I'd love to return it to its rightful owner."

No one said anything else about it, but David leaned in to whisper something in Kristy's ear. Sam and Nick sat next to each other stone-faced. Whatever conversation they'd had after the coffee mixer must not have gone well.

Frustration filled me. I felt no closer to answers than the moment I'd witnessed the murder. We had a lot of pieces and no way to connect them.

Max cleared his throat and spoke for a little while, apologizing for everything that had happened, while also thanking us for honoring him with our stay. It felt so trite and dishonest, that I clamped my lips shut and tuned him out until he made the announcement I'd been expecting since earlier.

"One more thing before I let you enjoy the main course. Due to inclement weather—"

He didn't get to finish his statement before the groans began.

"The manuscript viewing event is unfortunately canceled. If you'd like to receive a refund for the event, I'll connect you with my assistant who can handle that for you." Max smiled apologetically. "I will reschedule as soon as it's appropriate."

"Spring, hopefully," someone murmured. Several people laughed. Anger flashed in Max's eyes, but he smiled and dipped his head in acknowledgement. "Or at least earlier during winter, perhaps even fall."

"Does that mean we can leave?" Nick asked.

Max glanced at me, fury brimming in his eyes. "Ah, the police have asked everyone to remain for at least the next 24 hours. Besides, it's too dangerous to leave right now. We've had to move all the vehicles to higher ground."

Murmured conversation sounded as Max fell silent.

BOOK CLUB BAIT & SWITCH   155

No one looked happy about it, but no one argued either. Instead, they started haggling.

"How much of our stay will be comped due to this inconvenience?" Heath James asked.

Daniel laughed under his breath.

"At minimum, the last 48 hours," Temperance chimed in. She hadn't been super chatty either, but she and her husband had done nothing to rouse suspicion. "It's not every vacation where a murder and a separate physical attack occurs."

Nods of agreement all around.

"I think we should be more worried about a potential murderer walking among us than recouping money for inconvenience," Daniel drawled. "All of us have more than enough money to go around, so maybe we can focus on what really matters here."

David Brauer pushed his salad plate away and leaned forward. "And what exactly really matters?"

It was official. I couldn't stand a single person in this room besides Daniel. "An innocent woman was murdered. Another woman was seriously injured." I scoffed. "What is wrong with you people?"

"You people?" Mary said. She clicked her tongue. "Last I checked you are at this table, too. Doesn't that make you one of us?"

I took a deep breath and quelled the urge to storm out of the room. Hardy and Quinn needed more time. If I left now, it might get them caught. "No," I said quietly. "I'm not like any of you. In fact, I don't even know how Hardy got tickets to this thing."

"Err, I gave them to him," Daniel murmured.

I snorted. Of course he did. "Don't get me anything for Christmas, Daniel. My poor heart couldn't take it."

"Amusing as always, my dear."

Daniel took a sip of his white wine. "I think what Dakota is trying to say is we are all being particularly heartless today. These women are someone's daughters. Perhaps we could at least pretend to have some empathy and concern?"

"And if not that, isn't anyone else concerned about being next?" I said, frustration making my voice quiver.

"It's obvious what happened," Sam said.

My attention snapped to her.

She wouldn't meet my eyes. "Someone was having an affair with that woman—"

"Her name was Angela," I said.

"With Angela, and she tried to break up the marriage. Things...escalated."

Everyone in the room was staring at her. "And how do you know this?" I asked.

She sighed. "I don't, but I heard she was having an affair with someone here. It's pretty obvious the man snapped and attacked her. So, I guess the first step is to figure out who was having the affair and then go from there, isn't it?"

Daniel's smile sharpened. "I think it's much more difficult than that. I suspect 75 percent of the people in this room are having an affair."

I blinked and turned to Daniel. "What?" I hissed. "How could you possibly know that?"

Half the women in the room shifted uncomfortably.

Oh. My. Word. "You did not," I said under my breath.

"No, I didn't," Daniel said with a cheeky grin. "But it wasn't for lack of opportunity."

This was becoming a real-life Harper Valley PTA. I rubbed the space between my brow and reached into my pocket for my cell to text the only sane person in my life.

How's it going? This place is a nightmare.

Give us five minutes.

I could hold on for five more minutes.

I hoped.

The husbands seemed to catch onto what was happening. Less than a minute later, half the people were arguing. Max had a bewildered look on his face, and I was just sitting there, completely numb. This entire situation was so ridiculous I wanted to laugh.

Except a woman was dead and nothing about this entire vacation was funny at all.

"You need a girlfriend," I muttered to Daniel.

He sent me a side glance. "I had a promising lead on one, but it didn't work out."

"Please don't date anyone here, I beg of you."

"You don't have to worry about that."

We sat in silence and waited for everything to die

down, but two of the couples—Luke and Temperance and Chelsea and Cliff—rose.

I scrambled for my phone.

Two couples leaving. Hurry.

The response took a harrowing amount of time to come.

Done.

I sagged in my seat.

"Ready?"

Daniel nodded. "I've never been more ready in my life."

We rose and slipped out of the room.

HARDY AND QUINN were putting on their jackets when we walked into the room. Without a word, Hardy handed me mine and told Daniel to grab his.

"What's wrong?" I asked.

"We need to have a talk outside this mansion," Hardy said quietly.

Quinn was grim-faced and quiet.

Daniel took one look at us and turned. "I'll meet you in the kitchens."

"Do I have time to change?" I asked.

"Hurry," Hardy said.

I grabbed a pair of jeans, a heavy sweater, and a pair of wool socks and hurried into the restroom to change.

When I came out, both men stood by the door waiting. Hardy handed my scarf to me and opened the door.

BOOK CLUB BAIT & SWITCH   159

Daniel was already waiting for us by the kitchen doors. He asked no questions and followed us outside. Snow blew in violent flurries, but Hardy stepped into the poor weather and took me by the arm. "Stay close."

I huddled into him as he led us further into the grounds.

"Are we going to the greenhouse?" I asked.

"Quinn is going to sweep it for bugs and cameras," Hardy answered. "Say nothing until we're sure it's clear."

My heart started to pound. I nodded and fell silent.

The walk over only took a minute, but it felt like a hundred years. As soon as the door shut behind us, I stomped my feet and tried to blow some heat into my hands. Daniel stood off to the side of the room, silent and grim. Quinn took a small device with a blinking red light from his coat pocket and headed to the back of the room.

No one said anything, but Hardy came over and brought me into the circle of his arms. I buried my head in his chest, breathing in his fresh scent. My body shivered with cold and fear, and an underlying sense of dread had taken root inside me.

It took Quinn twenty minutes to go through the entire greenhouse and we stood in tense silence the entire time. When he finally came back, he nodded to Hardy once.

"Three. All disabled. We'll have a few minutes to speak before anyone realizes and they bring them back online. I wouldn't go more than five minutes."

Daniel moved closer to form a circle with our bodies.

Even without the threat of cameras, we stood close together and spoke in hushed tones.

"What is going on?" Daniel asked.

"The mansion is covered in cameras, so we have to assume the one we set up is compromised. I should have realized when there's been no indication of motion for days." He shook his head. "I found listening devices in all the rooms, including our own."

"Max has heard everything we've said?" I stepped closer to Hardy. He wrapped an arm around my waist and pulled me against him.

"We have to assume so," Quinn said. "While this is not an indication of guilt, it does point to some concerning tendencies of our host."

"Plus, it's illegal to have cameras in bedrooms when other parties using those rooms are unaware," Hardy added.

But both men were still very tense. "What else?" I asked.

"We found notes in Max's bedroom about everyone's comings and goings, our behaviors, things like that," Quinn said.

Daniel swore. "Like a real-life character analysis. What is his end game here?"

"It's novel research?" I asked, disgust filling me at the privacy violation.

"It has to be." Anger glinted in Daniel's eyes. "Every writer takes from real life, but to watch people on cameras and use those things to fuel your work is an egregious breach of privacy."

A terrible thought occurred to me. I stilled, and Hardy nodded as if he'd read my mind.

"Yes. With all that surveillance, there's no doubt in my mind Max knows who the killer is," he said.

"If he hasn't turned the information over, he's either protecting the killer or he is the killer," Quinn added.

"He's bound to have erased the footage," Daniel said. He closed his eyes for a brief moment. "I know we've jokingly spoken about this before, but I now ask this in all seriousness. Should we leave?"

Silence fell. I'd never walked away from a case in my life, nor had I ever truly been tempted. Until now.

"They can't legally keep us here," Hardy said. "They can pressure us, but we've documented everything. If they try to force us, I'll release every bit of information I have."

"I hate that he might get away with this." The thought bothered me to my very core. "Is there any way to recover the footage?"

Quinn shook his head. "Already called the forensic guy. His system overrides footage every thirty-six hours. It's already been recorded over."

"Dakota painted a large target on her back earlier by telling everyone she found a ring," Daniel said. "Everyone should be extra careful over the next twenty-four hours."

"Why the exact time?" I asked.

Hardy and Daniel exchanged a look. "Because that's

all I'm giving it," Hardy said. "If we can't tie this thing together in twenty-four hours, we are leaving and pretending we never met any of these people."

He sounded utterly sure in his conviction, and as much as it pained me, I nodded in agreement. "One day then."

"Never go anywhere alone," Quinn warned. "I've figured out where the cameras and bugs are in our room and was able to set up our own surveillance without giving it away. We'll know if anyone comes into our room. It's not connected to Wi-Fi, so Max won't be able to tell it's there. Be careful what you say, but don't be so awkward it rouses suspicion." He gave me a meaningful look that made me roll my eyes.

"Anything on the ring or buttons?" I asked.

"Nothing," Hardy said, "but we didn't have time to do thorough searches in anyone's room. If anyone was hiding an engagement ring box, he'd ensure his spouse wouldn't stumble across it."

"Nothing interesting in Nick or David Brauer's rooms?" It's not like they'd have a journal entitled *Ways I Broke the Law* lying on their nightstand, but one could dream.

"Nothing we found, and Max going to know we went into everyone's rooms very soon—if he doesn't already know," Quinn added.

There was one more tact we hadn't tried. "Does anyone know his assistant's name?"

Slow head shakes from everyone. "Has anyone seen her?" I asked.

"No, but we haven't been to his office yet," Hardy said.

Daniel interjected. "I can take care of this one. When I get back, I'll call Max and try to get him for dinner this evening."

"And if he brings up our snooping?" Quinn asked.

Daniel shrugged. "He's the one who sort of okayed you finding out what happened. I'll let him know that's how you're doing it."

"Because he knew the odds of us finding something are close to zero," I growled. "And now that he knows, he'll go to even longer lengths to prevent us from doing our job."

"Have you sent this info to Kevin?" Daniel asked.

"Not yet. This place doesn't have a great signal, and I disconnected from the Wi-Fi once I realized how deep his surveillance went," Quinn answered.

"Aren't mansions like this notorious for having hidden passageways?" I asked.

"Usually," Daniel said. "Mine has several. But if everything is wired, he'll know if you find them."

"Is there a way to temporarily disable his systems?" I asked.

"Yes, but who's to say he's not monitoring those passageways?" Quinn asked.

Daniel shook his head. "Doubtful, especially if no one else knows about them."

"First of all, we don't know about them. How on earth would we figure out how to find them?"

Daniel grinned. "I think I can help with that."

Quinn checked his cell. "Time's up. Let's get out of here."

With that, we braved the elements one more time and hurried back into what was quickly becoming a mansion of horrors for all of us.

SEVENTEEN

Max accepted Daniel's invitation to dinner. The rest of us decided to skip the formal dinner and throw ourselves upon the mercy of the staff and raid the kitchen.

Quinn oozed more charm than I'd ever seen and exited the kitchen with a full roasted chicken, a plate of leftover cake, and two food storage containers full of sides.

I gaped at his bounty and held out my hands to help him carry some of it. "What in the world? How'd you score all of this?"

Quinn snorted. "It's a shame you're the only one who fails to see my appeal."

"I can't see why, considering you're always so humble."

Hardy took one of the items from me and the cake plate from Quinn. "Let's get back before someone stops us."

We hurried back to our room with our feast and spotted Poppy curled up on the bed.

"There you are!" I exclaimed.

"She must have known we had food," Quinn grumbled. "I'm not sharing with you, feline."

Poppy cracked open an eye and meowed.

We ate and chatted for a while, and I relaxed for the first time since I arrived here. When we finished and had poured a second glass of wine, Poppy hopped from the bed and went straight to the door, looking back at us.

Quinn groaned.

"You should know better than to ignore her," I said lightly as I rose to my feet, careful not to spill my wine. "Maybe she found something helpful."

Hardy eyed the cat. "You have that tech person of yours on standby?"

A furrow appeared between Quinn's eyes. "I do."

"Send him a text and tell him to get ready."

Quinn shook his head. "If you ever tell him it was because of a cat, I'll disown both of you."

"Just being careful. Poppy has surprised us all more than once." Hardy rose to his feet, and we waited for Quinn, who grunted in annoyance before following.

When we opened the door, Poppy shot away like a rocket, glancing over her shoulder to ensure we followed.

"How long will we have once he takes the communication down?"

"He said the most he could give us is twenty minutes before people get suspicious. Since it's storming, maybe half an hour max."

BOOK CLUB BAIT & SWITCH   167

"Can he take it down for a couple of minutes, bring it back up, then do it again for longer?"

Quinn sent a text on his phone before looking back up. "Yes. Though he's very curious about what's going on."

Poppy stood at the entrance to Max's study.

I shot Daniel a message.

We'll be here for a while, he responded. *Do what you need to do.*

"Tell him to take it down," I said, a gut feeling growing in my stomach.

Quinn frowned but sent the message. Less than a minute later, he growled, "Done. Let's go see what this is about."

Poppy ran into the room, and we quickly followed. She passed through the main area and went into the space where Angela was killed. Without stopping, she ran to one of the back walls where a shelf overflowed with books and rose on her hind legs, swatting at something I couldn't see.

Hardy came forward and scooped Poppy up. She meowed and pawed at one of the books. With a snort of disbelief, Hardy pushed the book.

Nothing happened.

Poppy meowed again.

"Try pulling," I suggested.

Hardy did, and a soft click sounded from behind the shelf.

"I'll be a monkey's uncle," Quinn breathed.

The bookshelf cracked open, revealing a dark passage behind it.

"After you," I said to Hardy, not wanting to head down a dingy secret passage first.

"How chivalrous," Hardy drawled. He grinned and stepped inside.

Quinn followed, and I went in last, with Poppy at my heels.

Hardy and Quinn both carried small flashlights, clicking them on as soon as the door clicked shut behind us.

"I hope we aren't locked down here," I murmured, my voice echoing in the empty corridor.

"I'm sure the cat will figure it out if we are," Quinn whispered.

Poppy ran ahead of us, saving a baleful glare for him.

Hardy slowed and waited for me to grip his hand.

"Stay behind me," he said. We rounded a dark corner that opened up into a circular room.

Quinn swept the flashlight over everything. "Unused. No one's been down here for years."

"I doubt Max knows this is here." Hardy pointed his flashlight up at the ceiling.

I saw nothing interesting in the room. No discarded books or shelves or anything of significance.

"Let's keep searching." Hardy tugged my hand to follow.

We must have walked for half an hour before we came to an area with three doors and a path veering off to the left. No light filtered through from anywhere. If those flashlights went off, we would be pitched into complete darkness.

"Should we look for booby traps?" I whispered. This entire thing was feeling too Indiana Jones for my taste, but the adventurous part of me was intrigued.

"Worried about a giant ball coming down the path?" Quinn asked, lips tugging up in amusement.

"Or a pit of snakes," I muttered.

Hardy peered inside the small window of the first room. "Shelves and a long table."

Quinn looked in the windows of the second and third. "Same, but there's a cot in the third."

"Let's take a look in there," Hardy said.

Quinn tugged on the door, but it wouldn't budge. It took both men pulling before the door groaned and came open with a loud screech.

I winced. "Think anyone heard that?"

"Not unless we're right next to an occupied room, but I think we've gone down instead of up," Quinn remarked. "We should be safe."

"Should," I said dryly.

Hardy winked and poked his head into the room. I followed Quinn.

A thick layer of dust lay on the floor and covered every surface. The cot was older, made of solid metal, and held a thin cotton blanket and small pillow.

Several shelves stuffed with hardcover books lined the back wall. I picked one up, dusted the cover, and choked when I cracked open the cover and saw the front page.

The published date was 1784.

"Can I steal this?" I whispered.

Hardy's attention pulled from the cot. "What?"

"If no one has been down here in almost 300 years, is it okay to steal some of these?" My heart pounded with the thrill of discovery.

"I won't say a word," Quinn said. "This guy deserves to be robbed blind."

I laughed. "True, but it doesn't make it right."

"I've always had flexible morals when it comes to terrible people," Quinn confessed. "Maybe just take one and we can all pretend it didn't happen."

My gaze met Hardy's. Amusement twinkled in his baby blues before he shrugged. "I'm with Quinn."

I took the one I held and rummaged through the shelf for another. Two wouldn't hurt.

We left that room, my ill-gotten gains in my hands, and veered down the path. After walking for a few minutes, Quinn abruptly stopped.

"Lights up ahead," he whispered.

We crept forward. The men dimmed their flashlights until only the bare minimum glowed to let us see the path ahead.

Three small holes held pinpoints of light. We each took one and peered through to see Max and Daniel eating in a small, dimly lit room filled with bookshelves and mounted animals.

It was yet another study, this one reminiscent of a

mansion tour I took where the historical figure had been an avid hunter. Taxidermy had never been my thing. There was something about the eyes that always sent a chill up my spine. This wall reminded me of it. All types of different wildlife peered at the room with hopeless, glassy eyes.

I shuddered.

"How are your friends faring with finding out who did this?" Max said.

Daniel smirked. "I'm sure with your vast network of surveillance, you probably know more than me about how it's going."

Max tipped his whiskey glass in acknowledgment. "How'd you find them?"

The jerk didn't even try to deny it.

"I travel and rent a lot of homes, so I don't have to stay in a hotel. I carry a device that lets me spot cameras." Daniel sipped his wine. "It wasn't too difficult to figure out what was going on. Though the ones in the bedroom are creepy even for you, Max."

His eyes flashed with anger. "I've had a lot of theft in my home over the last year or so."

"You know it's illegal if you're renting your place out. Cameras aren't allowed in bedrooms or bathrooms."

"There are none in any of the bathrooms."

Daniel chuckled. "Glad to see you have some morals, old friend."

Max sighed and leaned back in his chair. "It's necessary."

"I assume this means you have them everywhere in the house and not only in the bedrooms?" Daniel asked.

"Everywhere," Max confirmed.

"Is there a reason you haven't turned the footage over to the police?"

Max grimaced. "There is no footage."

Daniel studied Max. "You don't have them in your other study?"

"I do."

"I'm afraid I don't follow then. Why wouldn't you have the footage of the crime?"

"It's been erased."

"By...you?"

"No." Max rubbed his chin and sighed. "It would have been erased within thirty-six hours anyway, but there's a suspicious blank spot during that time."

Daniel fell silent for a long moment. "Who else knows how to operate your security system?"

Max shook his head. "No one. I hired a company to do it. They're the only ones with the access code."

"Have you given that info to the police?"

"They never asked."

I shook my head in disbelief.

Daniel leaned forward. "You do realize how all of this makes you sound, don't you?"

Max blew out a disgusted breath. "I don't care what anyone thinks of me. I could retire right now five times over if I wanted to."

BOOK CLUB BAIT & SWITCH   173

"I'm sure you could, but don't you care that a young woman died here?"

"I didn't know her," Max said, sounding like a sullen teenage boy.

"Neither did I. But it doesn't mean she wasn't worth knowing."

From the expression on Max's face, I didn't think those two would be friends when this vacation was over.

Servers interrupted them by bringing another course. Hardy stepped away from the wall.

"He'll tell us the rest later," Hardy whispered. "Come on." He took me by the hand and led me further down the path.

When we were far enough away to talk again, Quinn spoke, his voice quivering with anger. "When we get back to Silverwood, I'm going to pry so deep into that guy's life, he's going to have to have surgery to get me out."

"I'll help," Hardy vowed.

We walked for a little while longer until the path abruptly ended in a stone wall. A faint light glowed from a small circle in the stone.

"Is there a room there?" I whispered.

"Only one way to find out," Quinn said.

They stepped to the door. Hardy peered through the hole, and I held my breath as I waited. When he stepped back, he nodded to Quinn, who pulled a gun I hadn't even noticed from his waistband.

"When did you smuggle that in?" I hissed.

"I never leave home without it."

My jaw dropped. "Yeah, well, maybe you should because what the heck, Quinn?!"

He wiggled his eyebrows at me and waited for Hardy to open the door.

We entered a room none of us had ever seen. Screens lined the entire back wall filled with flickering black and white video screens.

"Whoa," I breathed. "This seems like something right out of one of those crime shows."

Hardy's expression darkened. "He has eyes on every room in this house."

Quinn sheathed his weapon. "Does he have sound?"

Hardy frowned down at the whatever it was on the table below the screens. It looked like one of those DJ sound boards. All kinds of levers and buttons and blinking lights flashed at us, taunting us with zero labels on anything.

"No idea," Hardy said.

Quinn stepped up next to him and put his hands on his hips, staring down at the contraption. "Hmm. It's been a while, but let me see if I can figure this out."

"Been a while for what?" I asked.

"I was a DJ in college."

"Whaaat?" A startled laugh escaped me. "I can't see that. At all."

Quinn's lips thinned. "That's because you see everything in black and white."

I gasped. "I do not! I'm a reader. Everything is in color!"

He threw me a quelling look over his shoulder. "So, you're just judgmental toward me, then?"

I opened my mouth to argue, then snapped it shut.

Quinn chuckled under his breath and went back to studying the board.

Had I been a jerk to him all this time? He annoyed me, but I thought we had a familiar bit running between the two of us. He'd say something salty to me, and I'd say something salty back, but was I the one being mean to him? From his response, it seemed like it.

Ugh. "Quinn, I'm sorry."

His shoulders stiffened. Hardy turned and studied me, his face unreadable. He didn't seem angry, more like he was waiting to see where this was going.

"I didn't realize I was being mean to you. I...I guess I don't know you well enough, and that bothers me a little. So maybe we can try again? When all this craziness is over?" When he didn't respond, I sighed. "I think we got off on a rocky foot with the speed dating thing. Can we start over?"

Quinn held up a hand. "We can talk after this. Right now, I need to remember how to use this board so we can figure out how to spy on people."

I frowned at his back. That wasn't quite how I thought this would go, but he didn't seem angry anymore, so I guess it would have to do.

He adjusted a few levers to no avail. Hardy's gaze flicked back and forth and up and down, trying to watch all the screens at once.

I texted Daniel again, asking how it was going.

Still here. You almost out?

Found a room full of surveillance. Delay him as long as you can.

No problem. We still haven't finished our entrée.

I tucked my phone into my back pocket.

A hum of voices sounded when Quinn messed with the next lever. He abruptly pushed it down to zero volume. "I need to figure out how to adjust it one at a time," he muttered.

Hardy stepped away and let Quinn geek out over all the buttons. "You doing okay?" he asked.

"I'm ready to go home and soak in a hot bubble bath for two hours."

His eyes twinkled with amusement. "Me too." Hardy rubbed his jawline. "I've seen a lot of terrible things and dealt with a lot of terrible people in my time, but this one takes the cake."

"I've never seen more terrible people in one spot since I had to infiltrate a Colombian cartel," Quinn muttered, his focus still on the soundboard.

"Books are easier than people," I agreed, wrapping my arms around Hardy's waist. "How about we stretch out our honeymoon even longer?"

Quinn snorted.

"Six months?" Hardy murmured.

"You're giving me a huge raise, if that's the case," Quinn said.

BOOK CLUB BAIT & SWITCH   177

Hardy and I locked eyes. "Doable," Hardy said, lips tilting up in a smile.

"Could we stay gone that long with Izzy in school?" I wondered aloud.

"We can hire a tutor to travel with us. Kids rarely get enough cultural experiences in their lives. It's school and extracurriculars until suddenly they're adults, and then bam four years of college, and then bam again, they're in the workforce."

I blinked up at him in surprise and opened my mouth to argue on instinct, but it hit me...he was right. Izzy could do her education wherever we went. As long as she was learning, did it really matter where we were? And couldn't we teach her as we experienced the same things?

I slid a glance at Quinn.

He snorted. "If you're seriously thinking about it, you need to hire another investigator. I'm game to hold down the fort, but you can't leave me alone for that long and expect the same income."

"That's doable too," Hardy murmured. He brushed his lips over mine. "Let's talk about this again when we're out of here."

"Deal," I said.

"Eureka!" Quinn called. "Where do you want to listen first?"

EIGHTEEN

We spied on the dinner first. The last course had just been served, but one couple—Sam and Nick—was conspicuously absent.

"Where are they?" I murmured.

"We'll find them," Hardy assured me. "Let's listen here for a bit."

Most of it was innocuous conversation, nothing that mattered to anyone except for the couple involved. But we discovered a startling thing about his surveillance system. If someone was actively controlling it, you could zoom in and focus the sound on a specific area.

"How much do you think he spent on this?" I asked quietly.

"It's not only a surveillance system," Quinn said. "A lot of artificial intelligence was involved."

He stilled and looked over his shoulder. "You don't think..." he trailed off.

"Was it Max's voice?" Hardy asked.

"I—I don't know. I'd just met him a few minutes prior, and they were whispering." Frustrated, I shoved my hand through my hair. "No one's voice sounds familiar."

"Max isn't involved in education, is he?" Hardy asked.

Quinn shrugged. "Not that I know of, but there's no real way for us to be certain what he's invested in unless we run an extremely thorough background check."

"Let's do that when we get back," Hardy said.

"What if he's our guy?" I asked. "Shouldn't we do that before we leave?"

"It takes longer than twenty-four hours to get something of that magnitude back," Quinn said.

He focused on Kristy and David Brauer. "These are the tech people?"

"Yes." Neither of them looked happy with the other.

Quinn zoomed in. We fell silent and strained to hear their whispered conversation, even with the fancy technology.

"How could you?" Kristy hissed. "You promised, David. Never again. And then you take me on this awful vacation, and she's here?"

Hardy and I exchanged a look. "That was easy," I murmured.

Quinn peeked out the door to ensure no one was coming, quietly closing it when the coast was clear. "It's not enough yet."

"I didn't know she'd be here, and I encouraged you not to come," he hissed.

"Did she follow you? Did you tell her you'd be here?"

David's brow furrowed. Kristy scoffed and shook her head. "We'll discuss this later. There's one more course, and I am not stomping out of here in front of all these people."

"Heaven forbid you show any emotion," David said sarcastically. "And it's convenient how you're avoiding what you did."

Kristy shut her eyes for a second and visibly schooled her expression. I bit my lip to keep from smiling at her obvious annoyance. It wasn't funny, but I'd dealt with enough men in my time to feel her pain. "Just stop talking and eat your dessert, please," she said quietly.

"Fine, but I'm leaving after I eat this. I don't care about the last course." At that moment, more servers entered the doors and dropped off more food. We focused on those two for a while, but neither said a word to each other.

"Let's try to find Sam and Nick," I said. "But stay out of their bedroom. The thought of interrupting something intimate gives me the heebie-jeebies."

"I agree," Hardy said, flipping through the other video footage. Quinn periodically checked the door to ensure we were alone, and I kept in contact with Daniel.

"We have maybe fifteen to twenty minutes before Daniel and Max finish up," I said.

"There," Hardy said. Quinn messed with a few buttons and slides and focused on Sam and Nick. They stood in a long hallway, heads bowed together, deep in discussion.

"Why won't you tell me where you were?" Sam said quietly. "Have you done something?"

"Leave it alone, Samantha," Nick said, jaw tightening as he looked away.

My lips pressed together. Was anyone at this place who they said they were? Did everyone here have deep-seated secrets? I looked away from the screen and skimmed the others, my gaze snagging on Sarah, the editor, as she hurried down the hallway. Her long red hair triggered a sense of familiarity inside me, but I couldn't figure out why.

Curious as to why she was rushing, I skimmed the other screens to figure out where she was when she turned a corner and disappeared from view.

There. A man disappeared into a room, and Sarah rushed after him, turning the same way. My eyebrows went up. It could be nothing...

"Quinn," I said when I couldn't find footage of the other room. "This camera...where is the next one?"

He stood beside me as we tried to find what camera controlled the room they'd gone into. "There." He pointed to one on the far right. A deep chuckle rumbled his chest.

"Well, now we know who Kristy was so angry about."

Sarah and David were tangled around each other, sharing a passionate kiss. Sighing, I took out my cell and snapped a few photos of them. "I hate it here," I muttered under my breath.

"It's probably not David, then," Hardy said.

182   S.E. BABIN

"It still could be depending on how much energy he has," Quinn said.

"I don't even want to think about it." Looking away from the feed, I tried to find Max and Daniel.

"Bottom left," Quinn said. "They're finishing up, so we should get out of here soon." He adjusted the sound, but their conversation had turned to more idle things, so I found Sam again.

She and Nick had separated. Sam went back into her room, and Nick headed toward the kitchen area and paused by the door.

"Daniel and Max are leaving," Quinn said. "Let's get out of here."

"Where in the mansion will this dump us if we exit through this door?" Hardy asked.

Quinn pulled something up on his phone. "West wing. Daniel and Max are in the east. We should be fine as long as we don't dally."

"Let's take one more look at Nick," I said.

Quinn bent closer and swore. "He's heading straight for us."

"Surely he doesn't know about this place?" I wondered aloud.

Hardy and Quinn watched for a long moment. "Step into the passage," Hardy urged.

I didn't hesitate. Within seconds, all three of us were outside the room, peering in through the tiny holes disguised in the wall.

When Nick stepped inside the room, Hardy's jaw clenched. "Unbelievable," he whispered.

We watched as he expertly navigated the board, zooming in on one person in particular.

Kristy Brauer.

Nick watched for a couple of minutes before slipping out of the room. "Should we head through the tunnels or go out here?" I asked.

"I think it's safer to exit here. The signal will go down for a few minutes in about thirty seconds, so get ready to move," Quinn said.

"I need to meet this friend of yours," Hardy murmured. "Whoever it is could help a lot of our cases."

"If you two lovebirds leave me for six months, you'll be bringing him on board," Quinn said dryly.

"Fair enough," Hardy agreed.

"Let's move," Quinn said, opening the passage again. "If we run into anyone on the way back, claim we got lost."

I held my breath until we were safely out of the room and headed down the hallway. No one said a word until we were back in our room. Poppy had somehow gotten back into the room, so I scooped her up and kissed her on top of the head.

"Well, that was interesting," Hardy said as he sank onto the decorative chair with a groan.

We couldn't speak freely anymore, not after seeing the extent of Max's creepy surveillance network, but there was nowhere else we could go.

I sent them both a text message.

What if it's an affair and *a business deal?*

Quinn and Hardy's brows lifted as they read the message.

"Could be. How do you figure?"

Is there somewhere we can speak? This is annoying.

Quinn chuckled. "Not really."

I kept typing and explained my theory. Hardy skimmed the message and sat back in his chair, a thoughtful look on his face. "That makes the most sense."

Quinn nodded. "Who's hungry?"

Hardy and I both raised our hands and laughed. "The weather has calmed down. Maybe we can get something delivered."

Quinn shook his head. "No. We're going out. If I have to sit in this place for another minute, I'll scream."

"Who's going to drive in this weather?" Hardy said, craning his neck to peer out the window.

A wicked grin appeared on his face. "The FBI."

NINETEEN

Half an hour later, we were peeling out of Max's driveway like bandits. We'd all packed an overnight bag, ensuring we took our valuables with us. If we didn't come back, I'd be fine with leaving the rest of my belongings behind. Daniel sat sandwiched between Hardy and Quinn, and I was pressed up against the window next to my fiancé, holding Poppy's carrier.

"Hey, y'all," said the driver.

"Dakota," I said, giving him a friendly wave.

"Chet," he said. "Quinn and I go way back. Heard you're having some big trouble in that mansion."

"You could say that." I scooted closer to Hardy.

"This is Daniel and next to him is Hardy Cavanaugh," Quinn said. "Former law enforcement turned private investigator."

Chet winced. "Tough gig. You still have all the

instincts from before but none of the cool toys to help you with the job."

Hardy rubbed his temples. "We aren't even getting paid for this."

I stilled. "Oh, man. I forgot about that. Can we bill Max?"

"You bet we can." Hardy chuckled. "With a four hundred percent markup."

"And if he doesn't pay, I might have to lose those photos I took of his creepy surveillance room," Quinn added.

"I'm going to pretend I heard none of this," Chet said.

"Good idea," I said. "Where are we going?"

"How about steak?" Chet said.

"I'll take anything that doesn't come in four courses or requires me to dress up." We'd all changed into sweaters and blue jeans and donned all our winter gear. The weather had calmed down quite a lot since earlier, but the roads were almost empty. Few people were crazy as we were, but our escape was driven by desperation.

"Is there a hotel close? We need to drop Poppy off first." She was calmer than usual. Normally, she hated her carrier, but maybe even she was grateful to be out of that place.

"I'll take you to the one I'm staying at," Chet said, taking a left at the red light.

"How soon before Max tries to hunt us down?" Quinn drawled.

Daniel's phone rang. "Right now."

"Don't answer it," Hardy said. "Make him sweat."

He tucked his phone back into his pocket. "I feel like I should apologize," Daniel said.

A laugh cracked from me. "It's not your fault there was a murder on the premises."

"Yeah, but I knew Max was a terrible person." He grimaced. "Not that terrible, but he certainly isn't someone I hang out with much."

"There was no way to know it would skid off the rails this bad." I chuckled to myself. "What a nightmare."

Chet pulled into a well-lit parking lot full of vehicles. "Make sure you try their mac and cheese. It's spectacular."

HALF AN HOUR LATER, two servers approached our table with a mountain full of dishes. My stomach growled loudly as she set a heaping plate of chicken fried steak and sides in front of me.

"We should have stayed at a hotel and hit this restaurant up every night we were here. If I have to look at another unrecognizable vegetable with fancy garnish, I'm going to lose it." Quinn picked up his fork and dug in.

I had to agree. As much as I loved fancy food, few things compared to good ol' southern food, especially when it was fried.

Conversation was sporadic as we dug in, but when we finished, we ordered another round of drinks and laid out all of our evidence.

Chet, Quinn's FBI friend from Texas of all places,

proved surprisingly helpful, offering insights we hadn't thought about yet.

But, when dinner was finished, we all came to the same conclusion.

Either Nick, David, or Kristy murdered Angela. They all had motive. Nick refused to offer an alibi. David was having an affair, and Kristy was extremely angry about it. One of them was guilty.

We just had to prove it.

BACK IN OUR ROOM, Poppy lay curled on the loveseat next to Quinn. Hardy and I sat on the opposite couch, my feet in his lap. Daniel had gotten another room and said he was going to head out early tomorrow. In his words, "I'm an author, but even crime gets tiring sometimes."

The quarters weren't nearly as nice as Max's place, but we could speak freely, and we finally had privacy.

Or we would as soon as Quinn went back to his own room.

"I think it's Kristy," I said.

Quinn wrote something down on his notepad. "Weren't you there? Did you see a woman besides Angela?"

"No, but the library is large. It took me a while to get there."

"How long would you say? Thirty seconds? A minute?"

"Maybe 30-40 seconds," I said, thinking back. "Give or take a few. I didn't see a female running out, but she could have had time to leave."

"Maybe," Hardy acknowledged. "But he lingered?"

"Not when he heard me. He didn't even turn around."

"Has Kristy said anything odd?" Hardy asked.

"No, but doesn't the victim look a lot like that other woman, Sarah?"

Quinn's attention snapped up from his notepad. "You think it's a case of mistaken identity."

"I'm not following," Hardy said.

"David is having an affair with Sarah. We've proven this. Angela and Sarah resemble each other, and the room was dark. David works in tech, so what if he was trying to finalize a deal with Angela for her AI program, and Kristy had followed him in thinking he was seeing Sarah?"

"So, Kristy lost it when she saw her?" Quinn asked.

"Maybe. It makes sense," I said.

"If you're crazy maybe," Quinn muttered.

"There's no way Sarah knows," Hardy said. "If it happened that way, Kristy and David are keeping it quiet."

"They have to. Now he's an accessory," Quinn said.

"And the idiot is still sleeping with her." Hardy chuckled. "That's a man who likes playing with fire."

"He's rich," Quinn said. "There are no consequences for people like him." He gave us a thin smile and rose. "I'm looking forward to sleeping in my own bed tonight, so I will bid you adieu." Quinn gave us a little bow and left us alone.

Hardy let out a loud sigh and tilted his head back to stare at the ceiling. I moved my feet and snuggled against him, nestling my face against his chest. "I love you."

He tangled his fingers in my hair. "I love you more."

We sat like that for a while until he extricated himself and held out his hand. "Ready for bed?"

"Absolutely." I slid my hand in his and rose.

WE MET for breakfast the next morning. Quinn waved his cell when he saw us and grinned.

"Had to turn my phone off last night. Max is losing his mind."

"Dakota and I have a bet going. How many times did he call?"

Quinn glanced at me. "What was your number?"

"Twelve."

"Hardy?"

"Eight."

"Daniel said it was eleven," Quinn said. "Dakota wins."

"Any interesting messages?" Hardy asked.

"Blustering and threats. What time do you want to head back?"

"I figure we'd eat and stop by the local police station before we got on the road." Hardy shrugged his jacket off.

"I talked to Kevin last night. He's very interested in our Kristy theory, but it's still a good idea to stop by."

"I'm going to grab a cup of coffee and call Harper and

Izzy. Take your time. I'll grab lunch later on." I brushed a kiss against Hardy's cheek and left them just as the hostess showed up.

The hotel had a small business space, so I ducked in there to make the call. I was the only one there, so I decided to do Facetime first.

Mom answered on the first ring, her face way too close to the screen. "Darling! How's it going? It's so good to see your face."

We'd spoken via text, but she was right. Facetime was always better. "Hi Mom. Things are going okay. Everything okay there?"

"It's wonderful! Any time you two want to gallivant around the world, Izzy is always welcome to stay with us."

"Izzy better not be a spoiled little princess when we get home," I said.

Gran leaned over Mom's shoulder. "Don't you worry your pretty little head about that. Of course, she's a little princess!"

"And no candy after dinner."

Mom rolled her eyes. "Oh Dakota. We've both raised children, you know."

"I do, but a grandchild is a different animal. You can pack her up and send her home when she gets the sugar zoomies."

"That's right," Mom said. "Best kind of kid ever." But she grinned and winked. "Want to talk to her?"

"Sure do."

Mom called Izzy over and I melted when I saw her sweet little face.

"Dakota!"

"Hi, honey."

And soon enough we were immersed in a conversation devoid of any murder or mayhem, and it was the best conversation I'd had in several days.

I called Harper next. All was well with the bookstore, and Harper had taken messages for anyone who'd stopped by the agency while we were gone. Everything there was calm, and I suddenly missed that feeling with every fiber of my being.

And as I sat there, I realized that I wasn't happy doing what I was doing. I'm not sure I ever was. While investigating was thrilling, I had so much more to lose than I ever had. We were in over our heads, and everything we'd done had felt like pulling teeth. Was my life worth all this stress when I had the ability to change it?

Tears filled my eyes as I said my goodbyes to Harper.

As I sat in the lobby waiting for Hardy and Quinn to finish their breakfast, I made a decision. It would only work if Hardy and Quinn both agreed, but we'd find another way if they didn't.

A slow smile tilted my lips up.

TWENTY

"Do we have to go back?" I whined.

"Not for long," Hardy said, steering me up the steps to the front door.

The butler, or whatever he was, opened before we knocked and gestured for us to come in.

"How nice," I drawled. "I wonder how they knew we were here before we knocked?"

Quinn laughed under his breath. "Sassy to the end, Dakota."

"Let's find Kristy and get out of here," Hardy said quietly. "If we can't close this case today, we're leaving."

"Where's Kevin?" I asked.

"On standby. As soon as I send word, he and other officers will respond." Quinn held his hand up and crossed his fingers. "And then I can go back to my mundane existence of daytime naps and early bedtimes."

"Have you heard anything about Kathy?" I asked.

"She's improving. I think she'll be out in a few days."

We turned the corner and stood in front of our room. Poppy meowed plaintively.

"Trust me, I know," I murmured.

We opened the door and stepped in, only to see Max sitting at the small table. Hardy took a step in front of me. "Is there a reason you're in our room?" he asked, his voice sharp.

"I've had some concerning privacy breaches since you've been here," Max said, his eyes focused on Quinn, as if recognizing the biggest threat in the room.

He'd be wrong, but Quinn was the one carrying a weapon.

"Oh?" Hardy said. "That must be troublesome for you."

Max's lips twitched. "I'm here to ask you to leave. I've had the liberty of having my assistant pack your things, and your car is being pulled around."

I laughed. "This is the best news I've had all week."

Max's brows flew together. "Excuse me?"

"I'm happy to leave. In fact, there's nothing more I want to do." I held up Poppy's carrier. "Did you hear that? We're going home!"

Poppy meowed.

"You'd rather leave a crime unsolved than for someone to stumble on your creepy little surveillance network?" Quinn asked.

Fury flickered over Max's face. "Get out," he hissed.

"Our pleasure," Quinn said. He gave Max a mocking salute and held the door open for us to walk out.

Max didn't follow.

"It's our last chance," Hardy said under his breath. "We only have a minute to find Kristy and get her to say something to incriminate herself."

But we didn't find Kristy. We found Nick on the way out.

He stepped into the hallway and held up a hand. "I need to speak with you."

"Hurry. We just got kicked out," Quinn said with a grin.

Nick blinked in surprise. "What?"

"Max doesn't feel like our presence enhances his social presence." Hardy pinned him with a look. "But while you're here, do you want to tell us why you were in Max's creepy surveillance room?"

Nick's mouth opened in shock. "Um. Well." He rubbed the back of his neck. "I work in tech. That room is legendary among us. He had the place remodeled a few years back, and the blueprints were passed around to everyone in our industry."

So, Max's voyeurism was an open secret around town. That made this entire thing worse in a way. I winced. "Why were you in there?"

"Because I overheard Kristy and David talking." He looked over his shoulder to ensure no one was listening. "He was having an affair."

Quinn snorted. "That's your proof? I suspect everyone here is having an affair."

"Where were you that night?" I asked.

Nick's eyes flashed. "None of your business."

I rolled my eyes. "The fact that you won't answer is pretty telling. And you're here trying to deflect blame on someone else."

His teeth pulled away from his lips. "I did not kill or hurt anyone," he hissed.

"Then where were you?"

His jaw tightened. "I was in the screening room."

Hardy stilled. "During the murder, you were watching all those screens?"

Nick swallowed hard. "I was."

Quinn muttered a curse under his breath. "You saw the entire thing," he breathed.

Hardy let out a long, slow breath, but before my next blink, he had Nick shoved against the wall, one hand on his throat.

"Hardy!" I gasped, shock rooting me to the spot.

"I brought my fiancée to this godforsaken place where she witnessed a woman dying right in front of her three weeks before our wedding! And you're telling me you saw the entire thing and didn't say a word the entire time we were here?" Hardy's blue eyes flashed with rage.

"Hardy." I laid a hand on his arm. "I'm fine."

"I am not fine," he said through gritted teeth.

"I—I'm sorry. I—I didn't know what to do," Nick stammered.

"You didn't want everyone to know you're a creep," Hardy hissed, "so you were going to let a murderer walk to save your own skin. But then you started feeling guilty."

Quinn put a hand on Hardy's shoulder. "Let him go," he said quietly. "The police will be here in a few minutes." He tapped the top right of his chest where his FBI friend had wired him earlier this morning. We had him, but Hardy was so angry, he didn't care.

Hardy's nostrils flared. His hand flexed, but he let go and stepped away. Nick sagged against the wall.

"I—I'm going to sue you!" Nick blurted. His hands shook as he straightened.

Quinn stepped so close to him their noses almost touched. "If a hint of a lawsuit comes on the wind, I will ruin you," Quinn said quietly. "I don't care how much money you have, we have the entire weight of the FBI on our side. You don't actually think we believe this is the height of your perversion, do you? I'm sure if we dig just a little deeper, we could find so much more. Couldn't we, Nick?"

The smile Quinn gave him sent a chill down my spine. Nick paled and turned on his heels, practically running away from us.

The sound of sirens blared in the distance. Right before we made it to the front door, Kristy and David Brauer stepped into the hall.

None of us bothered to stop, but I nodded at her as I walked past.

"Best of luck, you two," I said.

She blinked, then frowned, and as she did, the sound of those sirens sounded much, much closer.

And even though this was the worst case we'd ever been involved in, the sight of her face growing pale as she realized why the police were here made me smile.

TWENTY-ONE

After some back-and-forth discussion, we sent Max an enormous bill for services rendered one week after returning home. As expected, Max abruptly responded with bluster about seeking legal options etc., etc., so we reminded him about our stay and what we found there. While we didn't resort to overt threats, this trip was such a nightmare for all of us we didn't believe Max should get off scot-free.

Within a few days we had a healthy wire transfer in our bank account and a formal letter banning us from his mansion. We framed that bad boy and hung it up in our office.

As far as the money? Hardy and I purchased very nice gifts for Fletcher and Harper for all their assistance with the wedding and beyond and gave Quinn a substantial bonus along with a formal contract for partnership in our business that he happily signed after a bit of back-and-forth negotiation.

The rest we dumped back into the business and hired Chet who swaggered in two weeks later carrying an old army duffle bag and wearing a grin. I didn't bother to check in about what happened once we left, but Chet had a lot to say once he finished setting up his work area.

Kathy and David immediately lawyered up. Nick tried to duck out and avoid the police, but I'd texted Sam on the way home to let her know what happened. She and I stayed in touch and while she hadn't said too much, things weren't looking so good on the home front for those two.

It was a case of mistaken identity on Kathy's part, and when Sarah found out she was the original target, she responded by filing a civil lawsuit. I didn't think someone could sue for an attempted murder that didn't happen, but I didn't press for details.

Honestly, I was just glad to be home, surrounded by people I loved.

Also, I lovingly banned Hardy from planning our next vacation.

Harper came in with a stack of books. She carefully did not look at Quinn and set them on the edge of my desk. "I read all of these last month and wanted to see if you wanted to order any of these for the shop."

I flipped through the titles and pulled out two after reading the blurbs. "If you feel strongly about any more, go ahead and pull the trigger on those, too. I trust your judgment."

Harper beamed as she scooped up the books. "Awesome. We've had a few authors reach out about signing events. I think one of them might do really well."

"Then book it." I smiled at her. "You don't have to bring all this stuff to me, you know. We've been working together long enough for us to trust each other."

"I know. I just want to make sure you know about everything going on."

"I appreciate that, but you don't have to include me in the decision-making process unless it's something way out of budget or has unusual circumstances. There's a reason you're a partner now."

She grinned and nodded. "Thanks, Dakota. Oh, Fletcher and I were chatting, and we wanted to run something by you. Give me a second. I need to grab it to show you."

Harper hurried away, and I pretended not to notice Quinn watching her go. "You ever going to ask her out?" I prodded.

He gave me a dark look. "She's still with that Jack character, right?"

I shrugged. "No idea. If she is, don't ask her out. But maybe let her know you're interested and see how she deals with it."

Quinn snorted and turned his attention to his screen.

Hardy gave me an exasperated look, and I shrugged. I'd never stop trying to get people together if I thought they made a good match.

When Harper came back in, she was carrying a

medium size box. After setting it down, she reached in and pulled out a stunning bouquet of beige and neutral colored flowers. But...they weren't flowers.

I glanced up at her. "What are those?"

"It's called Sola wood." She held the bouquet out to me.

It had sort of a crispy sound to it when I held it, but the flowers themselves were stunning. "The woman made it into a bouquet so you could see what it looks like arranged, but this isn't all we could do. You can dye the flowers whatever color you want, and they come in all kinds of varieties. It's much cheaper than buying fresh flowers, better for the environment, and you can keep it forever. Plus, you can scent them if you want."

I gawked at her. "That's—this is amazing, Harper, but it's only a few days until the wedding!"

Harper grinned. "Well, I took a huge gamble because I already booked it."

My heart swelled. Sometimes you had friends who just got you. Even though Harper thought she had to run everything by me at work, she knew me well enough to know I genuinely wanted someone to take most of the wedding stuff off my hands. "Oh, Harper. Thank you." Tears swelled in my eyes.

"You're welcome. I kept the same colors and types of flowers you already chose and sent those over to the designer. She already has most of them ready to go. I also requested special centerpieces for the head table and put together smaller centerpieces for the other tables." She took a breath and continued. "Fletcher took care of the bridesmaid flowers and the boutonnieres, plus special barrettes for Izzy and your mom and Gran."

Harper pulled out her cell and opened her photo album. "Here are a few of the things she came up with."

As I flipped through the pictures, I couldn't get over how realistic they looked. "This is wonderful. Mom is going to be so happy she can keep some of the flowers."

Hardy heard our conversation and came to peek over my shoulder. "Those are wood?"

Harper nodded. "Incredible, right?"

He laid a warm hand on my shoulder. "It really is. I've never heard of those before."

"Fletcher found them. Speaking of which, the rehearsal dinner is in a couple of days. She picked up your dress from the dry cleaners and wants you to get ready at her house. I'll be there, too."

"Uh. Okay. I'll have to see about that, but I'll try." I handed Harper's phone back and carefully put the bouquet back in the box. "I can't wait to see everything."

Harper grinned. "It's going to be beautiful." She picked up the box. "Holler if you need anything."

Hardy pulled out the chair next to my desk. "Best choice ever to help with this," he admitted.

I shook my head. "Maybe we should have gotten her a better gift."

He laughed. "She does it because she cares about you. Plus, you pay her better than any bookstore associate who ever lived."

"Yeah. But she deserves it."

The front door opened, revealing a small woman with a pale, drawn face. Chet rose and walked over, a friendly smile stretched across his boyish face.

"Well, hello, ma'am. My name is Chet. How can I help you today?"

Hardy and I watched as he made the woman feel at home before ushering her over to a seat at his desk. Satisfied he needed little help, we left it up to Quinn to monitor. When I brought up the idea of making Quinn a partner so we could travel more and possibly buy a second residence, Hardy hadn't batted an eye.

In fact, his shoulders had dropped, and he let out a huge sigh of relief. "You know, Dakota," he'd said, "I felt like hanging my hat up after this one. I think a break is just what we need."

"You and me both. How about we get married, extend our honeymoon as long as it's okay with Mom and Gran, and start shopping for a second home?"

He'd drawn me into his arms and kissed me stupid. So that was a definite yes.

Quinn came over to my desk and perched on the edge. "Why don't you two go on home? We have this under control. Enjoy your time before the wedding because it will get hectic soon."

"You kicking us out, Quinn?" Hardy said, amusement glimmering in his eyes.

"I'm trying to, but I don't have 51%, so I guess I have to ask."

Hardy laughed and lowered his voice. "So far Chet looks like a good call."

Quinn glanced over at his friend listening intently to the woman who was dabbing tears from her eyes. "Known him for years. Don't let the country bumpkin act fool you. He's an Army Sharpshooter and did some things in the service he refuses to talk about. I don't know a single agent sharper than him."

"I'm surprised he took the gig," Hardy admitted.

"Former military personnel are adaptable and love a new challenge. I'm not surprised at all." He rose from the desk and winked. "Plus, you waved a ton of money at him. Chet's dream is to have about two hundred acres of land and peace. More money is the way to achieve that dream."

Hardy and Quinn nodded in perfect understanding. "We'll get out of your hair then. Call us if you run into any issues."

"We can handle it." Quinn flicked his fingers at us. "Go take that bride of yours home. We'll see you at the rehearsal dinner."

I was already grabbing my purse. "You don't have to tell me twice!"

Hardy and I joined hands like we were teenagers and hurried out of the building.

MY PHONE RANG on the drive home.

"Ignore it," Hardy said immediately.

"Izzy is at Mom's. What if something happened?"

He sighed, making me laugh.

The caller ID flashed only the number, so I sent it to voicemail. I rarely answered my phone anymore if I didn't know the caller.

It rang again seconds later, so I did the same thing, but when it rang right after for a third time, I answered.

"This is Dakota."

"Miss Adair, this is Stephen Forrester. I'm a lawyer representing Kristy and David Brauer."

My grip tightened on my cell as dread soaked into my bones. "Yes?"

"They would like to speak with you about the events at Steinhoffer Mansion."

Hardy pulled into the parking lot of a grocery store and put the vehicle in park. He turned in his seat and listened, eyes keen on my face. His expression was grim but focused.

"Why?" I normally was way more loquacious on the phone, but there was no way I was saying more than the bare minimum to a lawyer, especially the Brauer's lawyer.

Stephen must have realized what I was doing. A friendly chuckle sounded over the line. "I can assure you it's nothing negative."

"I'll be the judge of that, Mr. Forrester, but you didn't answer my question."

"There are some...anomalies in the statements given to police and the evidence."

"I'm not sure how this is my problem."

Hardy grinned.

"It's certainly not, but your statements are different from everyone else's. My understanding is you and your fiancé are private investigators?"

"We are."

"Were you hired by Max to investigate?"

"Not technically."

"What does that mean?"

"It means Max was invested in figuring out what happened, but he never officially hired us. It wasn't until we made it to the end and went home that we issued him a bill for services rendered."

"And did he pay it?"

"He did."

Silence fell over the connection. "Willingly?"

I snorted. "Why don't you tell me what this is really about, Mr. Forrester?"

The sound of a shuffling and a door shutting sounded. "Can we speak off the record?"

Hardy held up a finger. I paused and waited while he set the record function on his phone. "We can, but Hardy is in the vehicle with me. Can I put you on speakerphone?"

"Good. I'd like to speak with him too."

I hit the speaker button. Hardy placed his cell close to mine.

"I'm merely trying to figure out what happened, Miss Adair. I am not a criminal defense lawyer, but I've worked for their family for years. They've retained me mostly for gathering evidence in an...unorthodox way."

"Which they won't be able to use for their defense," Hardy said dryly.

"While you and I are aware of that, surely you must realize that people who have access to the wealth that the Brauers' do don't always play by the rules."

"We're aware." It was impossible to keep the sarcasm from my voice.

"Yes. Well, I've seen the evidence against them and it's compelling. I've worked very hard to build my career in such a way that I can live with myself."

I blinked at the phone. An honest lawyer. Huh. You didn't meet a lot of those. Fletcher's brother was one, but to meet two in such a short time seemed against the odds.

"I wasn't a direct witness to the murder. I heard it happen and stumbled upon a male standing over Angela's body. I never saw Kristy there, nor did I tell anyone else I was there when it happened. They must have their own assumptions, but Hardy and my guests played dumb most of the time we were there."

Stephen made a mmm hmm noise. "And no one knew you were private investigators?"

"Sam did toward the end. Her husband did not have an alibi for his whereabouts during the murder."

"Is that Nick?"

"Yes."

"Interestingly enough, Nick's whereabouts are unknown."

Hardy's eyes shut. If they couldn't find Nick, the case against Kristy and David would probably fall apart.

BOOK CLUB BAIT & SWITCH 209

"Do you think he's still alive?" Hardy said.

I blinked. That thought hadn't even occurred to me.

"We don't know," Stephen said and sighed. "But it seems very convenient for a star witness to suddenly disappear, doesn't it?"

The reason for the call finally clicked. "You think they're guilty, don't you?"

"I can neither confirm nor deny. Part of my job is to field off any evidence about them. Positive or negative. And what I do with that evidence..." His voice trailed off.

This was just the case that kept on giving. "So, you don't know about Max's surveillance system?"

The pause told me everything. "Nick found out Max had an elaborate surveillance network and availed himself of it while we were at the mansion. He witnessed Angela's murder and kept it to himself."

"And he said Kristy was the one who stabbed Angela?"

"Yes."

"And now he's missing," Hardy said. "Funny how that happens."

"Yes, quite funny," Stephen said. "I've looked into your and your associate's backgrounds. You seem to be good people who've done their best to seek justice for those who can't seek it for themselves. I am merely trying to ensure I am not representing murderers. Even if it's not for the criminal case, I do not want my name associated with anyone accused of such a heinous crime. From this conversation, I can assume you are convinced of Kristy's guilt?"

"We can't speak about the evidence law enforcement

has. You'll have to get that from their defense lawyer, but in my professional opinion, Kristy Bauer was the only one who had the motive and opportunity to kill Angela. Her husband was having an affair with a woman who strongly resembled her, and Kristy mistook Angela for David's affair partner. Nick confirmed it and was an eyewitness." Hardy scrubbed a hand over his face.

"Why did you leave so soon?" Stephen asked.

Hardy and I both started laughing. "Max threw us out, but we were not sorry to go."

There was a long silence over the phone. "He threw you out?"

"He wasn't happy we discovered his extreme proclivity for voyeurism," I said.

"How extreme?" Stephen asked.

Hardy and I exchanged a glance. He shook his head once. "I'll just say when Max refused to pay our invoice, we reminded him about that network and how damaging it might be if former guests found out about it. We had our money within forty-eight hours."

Stephen sucked air through his teeth. "Got it. Yikes."

"Do Kristy and David really want to talk to us?" I asked.

"Oh yes," he said with a laugh. "I let them know it was a long shot."

"We have no desire to see anyone from Steinhoffer Mansion ever again. Plus, we're banned."

He barked a laugh. "I'm glad I called. This conversation has been eye-opening."

"A friend of ours got us tickets to the manuscript event, and it didn't even happen. And the thought process boggled my mind. Murder in the mansion? The event is still on! Bad weather? Cancelled!"

Hardy chuckled at my sarcastic tone.

"Instead, we got wrapped up in a murder and got stuck having awkward dinners with everyone each night." I sighed. "I've never been so glad to get home."

"I bet so. Thank you for speaking with me. I'd like to leave you with a warning, Miss Adair. I'm sure you've already noticed, but some people who hold extreme wealth hold a very high opinion of themselves. They do not believe rule or law applies to them. Be very careful over the next few weeks. I cannot guarantee Nick won't show up holding a grudge."

"If he's even still alive," Hardy said.

"And that's a big if," Stephen agreed. "Take care of yourself and best wishes on your upcoming nuptials."

At our silence, Stephen laughed. "It's no secret you two are getting married. Kristy and David mentioned it."

I let out a sigh of relief. "Thanks for calling, Mr. Forrester."

"It's Stephen, please, and thank you for speaking to me."

We hung up and didn't say a word for several seconds.

"You think he's still alive?" I asked.

"I don't know what to think," Hardy murmured. "We need to call Quinn and Daniel to update them."

"I'll call Daniel. He's been dodging us."

Hardy chuckled. "I think he feels guilty."

"As he should," I growled. But I wasn't mad at him. No one could plan for the sheer level of craziness we experienced at that mansion.

Hardy started the vehicle and got back on the road. "What time is your mom dropping Izzy off?"

"Around four."

"Good," Hardy said, his eyes brimming with heat. "We're going to be busy for a little while when we get home."

Heat bloomed on my cheeks.

TWENTY-TWO

Daniel popped by the house after Mom dropped Izzy off. He held a bottle of wine in one hand, a bag of food from my favorite Italian restaurant in the other, and an apologetic smile.

Izzy launched herself at him and wrapped her arms around his waist, pressing her face into his stomach. "Mr. Daniel!"

He laughed and bent down to hug her awkwardly. I took the food from his hands so he could scoop her up. "Hey kiddo. I heard you had a great time with your grandmas?"

She nodded. "We played dress up every single day!"

"Wow," Daniel said solemnly. "Were you the princess every time?"

"Yup!" Izzy said happily.

Hardy walked over and extricated his daughter from

Daniel. "Come on, kiddo. Looks like Mr. Daniel brought dinner for all of us." He eyed him. "Fettuccini?"

Daniel laid a hand over his chest. "I'd never forget Izzy's favorite dish."

"Yes!" Izzy shouted, throwing her fist into the air.

Poppy came out of her hiding spot and wove in between Daniel's feet. She'd made herself scarce over the last couple of weeks. I think the mansion experience might have drained her more than it did us.

Fang followed her out and pounced on Daniel's feet. His greetings were always spicier than Poppy's and sometimes ended up with claws in fabric. But Daniel had a soft spot for the clawed beastie. He scooped him up and held him at eye level. Fang stared.

"I hope you were good while we were gone."

Fang meowed.

I rolled my eyes. "Liar. He was a holy terror to Harper."

"Well, it's good you're cute," Daniel said. He put Fang down on his bed and washed his hands before helping me dish out the food.

With Izzy's presence, we kept our conversation on mundane topics, but once we put her to bed, Daniel had kicked his shoes off and made himself at home.

One of Hardy's eyebrows rose. Daniel laughed. "Sorry. It's been a long day."

I waved a hand at him. "You know you can make yourself at home."

"First, I want to apologize."

"There's no need," I said.

"I know it wasn't my fault what happened, but I should have chosen something else for you two." He sighed and shook his head. "Something more fitting for your personalities."

I stared. "I'm not sure if I should laugh or be offended."

Hardy settled next to me on the couch.

"What I mean is our worlds aren't the same."

Hardy glowered.

Daniel snorted. "I'm screwing this all up." He lowered the chair and leaned forward, placing his hands on his knees. "You two don't put on airs. You're genuine and humble, and I cherish our friendship."

"Better," I drawled.

He rolled his eyes at me. "Aaaaand," he continued, "I should have known you wouldn't enjoy spending time with anyone there." He held a hand up. "Now, I had no idea who would be there, but I figured it would be people who appreciated books as much as you did. Instead..." he chuckled, "instead you got exposed to the worst of us, and I'm truly sorry about that."

"I think you're the same as us, Daniel," I said quietly. "I guess I don't understand why you hang out with those kinds of people."

"My family. It's all I grew up with. But I cherish our friendship. I hope you know that."

"Of course we do," I said, poking Hardy in the ribs. "Even if he acts grumpy about it."

Daniel looked at Hardy, his expression growing somber. "And I owe you an apology too."

Hardy frowned. "For what?"

"Needling you about Dakota. I want nothing more than her happiness, and she's found it with you. She... spoke with me about my behavior, and I took some time to reflect on my behavior. I understand if you would like me to limit my visits."

Hardy stared at him for a long moment. "I don't mean this to be cruel, Daniel, but I never worried about you stealing Dakota from me."

Daniel blinked. "Not even once?"

The grin he gave Daniel sent a shiver down my spine. "Not even once," he confirmed.

Daniel sat back and let out a huff of laughter. "Well, that's settled, I suppose."

I changed the subject away from us and told him about Nick. Daniel's expression grew grim as I spoke, and when I finished, he sighed. "I'll have someone look into his whereabouts."

"Quinn is already doing it. If he's still alive, we'll know something soon."

I looked at Hardy in surprise. "When did you do that?"

"Right when we got home. I'm surprised it's taken Quinn this long to find him."

"I plan to contact Max, too," Daniel said. "I'm sure he'd love to hear from me." He winked. "After all, I did bring in the riffraff."

"And here I thought we were making up," Hardy drawled.

"Let us know what he says. I'm going to call Fletcher and Cole, too. Maybe they can put something in the paper about Nick. It may discourage him to keep away from here."

Daniel's gaze darkened. "You really think he'll come here?" He shook his head. "If he were smart, he'd keep running."

"Technically, he's only a witness right now. There's no crime to detain him for. He can do what he wants."

The words were casual, but the tone told me exactly what he'd do if Nick happened to show up here.

"He's retired, correct?" Daniel asked.

"That's what Sam said. He invested well when he was younger." I needed to text her soon.

"What if those investments tanked?" Hardy mused. "If they did, Nick needed money. Fast."

I thought about it. It made a horrible sort of sense. "You think he was blackmailing Kathy and David for his silence." I rubbed a hand over my mouth and let out a stunned little laugh.

Daniel tilted his head. "That sounds exactly like something those people would do. But when we got involved, Nick knew we were close to figuring things out and decided to save his own skin."

"Maybe Kathy and David had already paid him, and Nick stabbed them in the back. It's not like you could enforce an NDA on a murder." I frowned. "Could you?"

"I'm no lawyer, but I bet you could finagle one about the details surrounding said murder," Daniel said.

A headache was beginning to form right between my eyebrows. "This keeps getting worse and worse," I muttered.

"The only thing that might draw him here is anger," Hardy said. "We didn't do anything wrong, but criminals have never been known to be reasonable. He may see us as the thing that took his guaranteed payday away."

"One more thing to worry about before the wedding," I quipped.

"Fletcher and Harper have it all in hand," Daniel said.

I eyed him. "How do you know that?"

His eyes sparkled. "I'm in the Dakota and Hardy wedding group text thread."

A horrified laugh bubbled from my lips. "You are not! I'm not even in that thread."

"I know." Daniel grinned at my expression. "Don't worry. It's all innocent. You chose your wedding party well."

"Is Quinn in that thread?" Hardy asked.

Daniel rolled his eyes. "Yes, but he put us all on silent because, and I quote, 'I don't give a bleep what color Dakota's shoes are. All of you need hobbies.' The man truly is a Neanderthal sometimes."

"I am not sure what to say."

"Say nothing," Daniel said, rising to his feet and stretching. "Just don't wear flats on your wedding day. Bring them with you and put them on at the reception."

My look of dismay made him snicker. "Fletcher's advice, not mine. But I agree with her." He shrugged his jacket on and headed toward the door. "On a more serious note, be careful. I'll call a few contacts and be in touch. See you at the rehearsal dinner."

When the door shut and we were finally in silence, Hardy blew out an annoyed breath and said, "Our friends have a group text about us?"

THE REHEARSAL DINNER arrived with little fanfare. All was quiet on the home front, and there'd been no sign of Nick. To my surprise, Kristy and David Brauer were still locked up. Being a billionaire didn't help this time, a fact I couldn't help but be pleased about. Bail wasn't normally granted with a murder charge, but the people at that mansion seemed to live by different rules than everyone else.

Poppy wore an adorable pink bow. Fang sat next to her wearing a black one. They stared up at me with rapt concentration. "If you get into your carrier without clawing my dress, you'll each get two snacks. Got it?"

Poppy turned and showed me her butt, her tail high in the air. But she crawled right into her carrier, turned, and curled into a ball. Fang turned to look at her, then back at me. He made no move to climb in.

I tossed two snacks into Poppy's carrier and shut the door. Fang screeched like I'd done him a great disservice.

"Sorry. You have to go in there like Poppy did. Once you do, the snacks are all yours."

Hardy's cologne drifted to my nose a second before warm lips pressed against the top of my shoulder. "You assume he's as sharp as Poppy."

I clicked my tongue. "Don't be mean to our baby holy terror. He's smart. He just doesn't know it yet."

Hardy wrapped a hand around my waist and pulled me against his chest. "You look beautiful." He buried his nose in the crook of my neck. "And smell like cotton candy."

"Thank you, but I'm involved in a highly delicate cat training situation. I'm afraid you'll have to wait a little while before I can reciprocate."

Hardy chuckled. "Weirdo," he said fondly before releasing me. "I'll need your help with this tie when you've given up on Fang."

"I'll never give up on you," I said to the cat.

Fang was completely uninterested in my words of encouragement. He only had eyes for the snack bag.

Izzy skipped out from the bathroom twirling a hairbrush. No matter what she wore, she was adorable. Today, she wore a blush skirt with black tights and a black fuzzy sweater with blush and black boots. Her hair was unbound and half curly and not finished based upon the startled shout coming from my mother who was still in the bathroom.

"Whatcha doing?" she asked, coming over to stand beside me.

"Trying to get Fang into his carrier."

"Did you try picking him up?"

Kid logic. Izzy - 1. Dakota - 0. I laughed and shook the snack bag. "I want him to get into the cage by himself so I can reward him. It teaches animals that if they do what we want them to, there's something positive in it for them."

"Is that why Poppy eats all the time?"

Hardy barked a laugh.

"Well, I tend to spoil her a little, but she's good at doing what I ask—"

Hardy cleared his throat. Loudly.

"So, I reward her a little more than I should."

"She's getting a little chunky," Izzy observed.

Mom came out of the bathroom waving a curling iron. "Izzy! I'm not finished with your hair!"

"Grammy, I don't want to. Can I just go like this?"

Mom's expression turned exasperated. "We can't leave the house half finished, Izzy. I promise, we're almost finished. Five more minutes. Then we'll put your hair up in a pretty bow and pearls, and you'll be all done."

Izzy's expression turned calculating. "If I do what you want, does that mean I get a treat, too?"

I pressed my lips together to keep from laughing. Hardy ducked into the bedroom and shut the door.

Mom shot me a dark look, but I stayed silent. She crossed her arms and looked up at the ceiling as she pretended to think. "If you come back into the bathroom and let me finish your hair, and make sure your shoes and jacket are ready, and be on your best behavior tonight, then you can have two pieces of cake instead of just one."

My eyes widened, and I opened my mouth to rebut it, but Mom lifted an eyebrow in challenge. I blew out a breath.

Izzy gasped like we'd just told her she was going to Disney World. "Okay!" She ran back inside the bathroom. "Hurry up!" she called.

Mom rolled her eyes and shook the hairbrush at me. "You deserved that," she whispered. "Just call me karma."

"I'm going to ask her if she wants to have a sleepover with you tonight after she gets through with the second piece of cake."

Mom narrowed her eyes. "Mmm hmm. You're lucky I love you."

"Grammmmmmyyyyy!" Izzy called.

"Have fun, Grammy!" I waved at her.

Mom snorted and turned to help Izzy finish taming her hair. Thank heaven she knew how to do all that fancy stuff. She tried to teach me when I was young, but I never had the patience for it. I'd kept my hair in the same style for years before I worked up the nerve to change it. It drove Mom crazy, but since it wasn't a mandatory life skill, she settled for buying my ponytails and barrettes, and I did the rest.

To this day, if it required more effort than a curling iron, I was out.

Fang still sat before me eyeing the snack bag.

"I don't have a lot of time. Either you get into the crate

and get a snack, or I'm going to put it away and put you in there myself."

Poppy hissed, a startling sound.

Fang jerked around, his fur standing high on his arched back.

They stared at each other, feline to feline, communicating in some way I wasn't privy to. Fang meowed, and Poppy hissed again before the younger cat turned around, gave me a long look, then hurried into his carrier, turned around and lay down.

"Supernatural cat," I whispered to myself. "But thank you."

I crouched down by Fang's carrier. "You're a very good boy," I said as I dug two treats from the bag and put them inside. Once both cats were secured in their carriers, I went to grab my coat and shoes.

Hardy sat on the bed, amusement curving his lips when I walked in.

"Hush, you."

He grinned. "She's caught me like that a few times, too." Hardy opened his arms, and I stepped into the circle, twining my fingers through his hair. He pressed his cheek against my abdomen and inhaled. "Are you ready?"

"Are you?"

"As long as it's with you? Always."

My heart warmed. "Ditto," I whispered. "Mom and Izzy are almost finished, and FYI, she gets to have two pieces of cake tonight."

I felt his wince against my stomach. "Hope you're ready for a late night."

"I hope we get the cake early and the DJ goes long into the night, so she wears off the inevitable sugar high."

"One can dream."

We sat there together for a long time, breathing each other in before there was a soft knock on the bedroom door. "Dakota, honey, we're ready if you are. Gran is meeting us there."

"Out in a minute, Mom!" I stepped out of Hardy's arms and hurried to get my shoes from the closet.

Hardy waited for me by the door and held out his hand. "Come on. Let's go pretend to get married."

TWENTY-THREE

We dropped the cats off at the boarding place for a couple of days, though we planned to take them with us when we left for our honeymoon. The paperwork for that had not been fun. Once they were all settled into their overly large room filled with cat toys and climbing trees that we had vastly overpaid for, we headed to the restaurant.

The gathering was relatively small, filled with people we loved. Fletcher was there with Cole. Harper and Jack, Mom, Gran, some of Hardy's family, Izzy, Daniel, Quinn, and even Chet had made it. We sat at one long table, Hardy at the head and me sitting to his right. Quinn sat opposite me. Harper sat next to him, and the choice surprised me, but neither seemed bothered by it.

For the first time in several weeks, I relaxed. All the work we'd done had culminated in this, the man I love sitting by my side, and both of us ready to commit our lives to each other. I reached over and took his hand.

He squeezed my fingers. Quinn was chatting with him about something related to the suits they'd ordered, so I didn't interrupt. Izzy sat between Mom and Gran, charming them like always. Fletcher and Cole had their heads dipped together, earnestly discussing something.

As long as it wasn't my choice of footwear, I didn't care.

She looked up and caught my eye, smiling when she noticed me staring. I smiled back and nodded to Cole. He winked and saluted me with his champagne.

All these people were here because of us, and the thought filled me with love and warmth. I was officially about to be Izzy's mom and Hardy's wife. Things were changing fast, and instead of being panicked about it, I felt the future open wide.

I was ready to step into it.

"Are you okay?" Hardy murmured in my ear.

"I'm wonderful. Just think. Tomorrow, we're going to be married."

"Mrs. Dakota Cavanaugh. I like the sound of that." He rubbed his thumb over the top of my engagement ring.

I groaned. "I'm going to have to change so many documents. What a nightmare."

He tapped the top of my palm. "You're only going to have to do it once, and I'll help you."

"You better," I muttered. "I've had paperwork coming out of my ears lately."

Quinn leaned forward. "I've got some buddies who might be able to get it done faster."

"I'm finally glad we hired him," I said.

Quinn grunted. "Careful, Dakota. That last case was a doozy, and you haven't gone on your honeymoon yet. I'd hate to have to take some mental health days."

"I take it back," I said.

Hardy took a sip of his wine. "Can you two cool it just this once?" His voice sounded amused, but Quinn and I turned the conversation to other things, but not before I stuck my tongue out at him.

The night passed by full of love and laughter, and when dinner was finished, we practiced walking down the aisle together. Technically, we didn't need this dinner since we had a small affair planned. It wouldn't be the end of the world if someone messed up walking down the short aisle. It was mostly an excuse to get everyone together one last time before things changed.

And I knew they would change because I'd put the wheels in motion already. Hardy, Izzy, and I were due for a long vacation. Life was too short to live your life the way everyone else thought you should live it, and in a few days, we were going to put our money where our mouth was.

Mom had retired a couple of months ago, and Gran filled her days with yoga classes and volunteer work. Both of them were ready for a change of pace. We wouldn't be gone forever, but we would be gone long enough to change our lives.

Hardy hadn't told his family about his upcoming sustained absence. When I questioned him, he'd grunted and said they wouldn't understand before telling me he wouldn't have understood until he met me and realized we were meant to be together.

But out of all of us, the one who most needed this was Izzy. She had stability with her mother before it was harshly yanked away, and she'd gone to live with someone she barely knew. And while things were much different now, we thought it was only fair to give her the opportunity to explore the world while she was still young and free of responsibilities. We still hadn't hired a tutor, but we'd get to it soon.

"You have to step with your left foot first, Dakota," Fletcher chided. "Like this." She glided along the restaurant floor like an angel while I rolled my eyes.

"Left. Got it."

She snorted. "I know you just want this to be over but trust me. If you step with your right and Hardy steps with his left, he's going to trip over your dress."

I didn't believe her, but if the left foot was that much more important than the right, I suppose I could try to behave.

We practiced for another hour and a half before I held a hand up. "Done! How about dessert?"

Izzy pumped a fist in the air. She ran over and hugged me around the waist. "I hope they have chocolate cake," she said against my skirt.

"We ordered a few different kinds, honey."

"Best dinner ever," she whispered before letting me go and running back to her seat.

The DJ was on the makeshift stage finishing his set up

while everyone took their seats. I found Hardy and gestured at him, jerking my thumb over my shoulder to tell him I was headed to the ladies' room.

He nodded and turned his attention back to Fletcher and Cole. By then, the restaurant had warmed up considerably, so I shrugged my wrap off and left it on my seat before walking to the back.

A quick glance in the mirror while I was washing my hands made me frown. Even the carefully applied makeup couldn't hide the shadows under my eyes from stress and lack of sleep. We'd been back for a while now, but there was still a pall over us because of Nick and the fallout from that case.

I only hoped a few months on white sand beaches and crystal blue waters could chase the blues away.

When I stepped out of the bathroom, I felt a soft wind at my back that I assumed was from the door, but a gloved hand holding something went over my shoulder and pressed against my mouth. I inhaled to scream only to get a mouth and nose full of something sweet.

My eyes widened, and I struggled against whoever it was, kicking out. My heel struck something hard, landing a grunt from the person behind me, but I wasn't fast enough. My limbs grew heavy, and my eyes slowly fluttered shut until darkness was the only thing I knew.

I WOKE up blind with a splitting headache. A gasp escaped me as pain bleated through my head when I tried to turn it. My arms were tied in front of me, but the blindness I realized with stark relief was due to a scarf tied around my eyes.

Something warm and metal rumbled underneath me. A vehicle. I was on the road being taken to heaven only knew where. I moved my feet, thankfully unbound, pulling my knees up close to my chest and bent my head to rub my face against my knees, slowly working the scarf off my face. The area was too large for me to be in a trunk. Maybe a camper or some kind of work truck.

After a minute of awkward posturing, the scarf slid up my forehead, but that was all I could move it without straining my neck. I looked around, shivering at the freezing air.

I was in a mostly empty truck, about the size of one of those old ice cream delivery vans. A small pile of boxes sat to my right labeled Tech Titan LLC.

If I could get my arms free, I could dig through those boxes to see if they contained anything to help me get out of this situation. I'd left my phone at the table, so there was no way for me to contact anyone.

For a moment, I gave in to the panic bleating through my veins, allowing myself a very short time to cry, but I had myself under control within a minute or two, and squared my shoulders, refocusing my thoughts to come up with a plan. My gaze skimmed the truck quickly, and then did a second, slower sweep to see if there was anything I could use to get free of my bonds.

My gaze snagged on a hook on one of the side panels

on the wall where truck drivers secured cargo prone to sliding. Maybe I could slide that hook into one of the loops in these ropes and loosen it enough to get myself free.

With a grunt, I rose to my knees and crawled over to it. My teeth chattered with cold, and my hands were numb with it, but it would be so much worse if I let myself stay bound and this truck stopped. I rose up, holding onto the hook to help me rise to a standing position.

With a slow, steadying breath, I went to work.

TWENTY-FOUR

It took a good fifteen minutes to work myself free, every second dragging like hours before I figured it out. And finally, finally I felt that last blasted knot tug free. I didn't worry about the boxes at first. Instead, I crept to the door and tried to tug it open, just in case the culprit got a little too cocky and left it unlocked.

No dice.

With a muffled curse, I hurried over to the boxes and opened the first, hurriedly digging through it to see if there was anything of use.

Nothing.

The second one yielded little either, but the third revealed a stash of brand-new cell phones and something metal and heavy. No idea what it was, but I could swing it, and that was good enough for me.

One thing I knew was you could call 911 on any cell phone no matter if it had a service plan yet, so I opened the first box, whispered a prayer, and powered it on, holding my breath and simultaneously praying it held a charge.

Even though the battery line was in the red, it powered on.

"Thank you," I choked and dialed emergency services.

Hearing someone else's voice made my throat tighten. "My name is Dakota Adair. I've been kidnapped."

The operator asked for a location, but I had no idea where I was and told her so. "My fiancé is former law enforcement. Is there any way you can connect me to him?"

"I'm sorry, ma'am. I need to stay on the line with you so I can trace the call, but you can give me the number, and I'll have another operator contact him."

I rattled it off and stayed on the line. "I don't have much battery left, but there are several other cell phones I can use to call back."

"You're in a work truck?" the operator asked.

"No idea, but the boxes say Tech Titan LLC."

"I'm going to place you on a brief hold, ma'am. Please stay on the line."

The truck was coming to a slow stop. I hurriedly unwrapped another cell phone and shoved it down the front of my dress. I still wore my heels, but I kicked them off. It was freezing outside, and those shoes would only slow me down if I had to run.

Whispering a prayer, I kept the cell to my ear and reached for the heavy box I'd found.

Soon, the truck stopped completely, and I heard the

door open. My heart pounded in fear. I needed the element of surprise, so I dashed for the rope and hurriedly wrapped it around my wrists in a haphazard circle, and pulled my knees up to my chest to hide what I held. I crooked my head against my shoulder to keep the cell phone on. If I heard keys in the lock, I'd hide it, but for now, this was a lifeline.

"Ma'am," the operator said when she came back on the line. "We're dispatching officers to your location."

"Did you reach my fiancé?" I whispered.

"Yes, ma'am. He's been informed."

"Thank you. Someone is coming. I need to hang up."

"No. Don't hang up! Hide the phone if you can."

"I'll try. Don't speak, okay?"

The woman's voice was tense. "Officers are less than three minutes out."

A lot could happen in three minutes. "Thank you," I whispered again. "He's unlocking the truck. I'm hiding the phone." I hurriedly tucked it into the waistband of my tights and re-wrapped the loops.

The back of the truck door slid open revealing Nick and another man I'd never seen before. I swallowed hard, unable to hide the tremor shaking my body.

Nick looked as nervous as I did, but he swallowed and slid a look over to the man. "This is her, the one who ratted out Kristy and David."

"I did no such thing," I snapped. "You ratted them out to us!"

Nick released a nervous laugh. "Don't listen to her. She's just scared."

The man gave him a dead look and climbed into the back of the truck. I scooted back against the wall. "Don't touch me," I whispered.

He didn't respond, only hauled me up by an arm. Saying a mental prayer, I lifted my other arm, the rope falling away, and swung that box as hard as I could, hitting him directly in the nose.

A crunch sounded, followed by a furious roar. He dropped my arm, and I lunged forward.

Nick screeched like a teenage girl and lurched out of the way, not bothering to stop me as I flung myself out of the truck and onto the frigid parking lot.

I had no idea where I was, but the lot was well lit. A mostly deserted gas station by the looks of it. He'd driven long enough to get me out of town. The road wasn't too far away, so I veered toward it, hissing at how cold the ground was, telling myself it was a temporary pain. If I stopped, it would be much worse.

I clutched that metal box like a lifeline, running faster than I'd ever run in my life. Tears streamed down my face, sticking to my cheeks because of the cold. I had no shoes, no jacket, and no money or wallet, and if someone stopped for me, I'd have to take a massive gamble. The devil I knew or the devil who might save me.

Nick shouted in alarm. "She's getting away!"

I didn't hear what happened after that. Instead, I darted across traffic and onto the other lanes that would hopefully take me back the way we'd come. There were very few vehicles out tonight, and they were way too far ahead of me for me to get my hopes up.

The tinny sound of a voice coming from my chest alerted me to the 911 operator still holding on.

"I'm running," I barked. "No idea what direction I'm going."

The woman's voice was low and urgent. "Do you see a road sign?"

I focused ahead of me. "I-114. West," I said with a sob.

"You're doing well. Don't stop ma'am."

The sound of heavy footsteps came through the brush.

Headlights approached on the other side of the road, so I darted back the opposite way, waving and screaming. They were probably too far away to see me, but I kept it up anyway, running faster than I'd ever run before. My breath tore through my throat, and there was a stitch in my side, but I was dead if they caught me.

A few awful seconds later, those headlights flashed. A broken cry tore from my throat. "Please be Hardy, please be Hardy," I repeated like a prayer.

More headlights came from behind, these with flashing blue and red lights.

I sped up and darted over the road once more, hurrying toward those vehicles.

The footsteps sounded even closer. A gust of wind came at my back, the feeling of fingers sliding grasping for loosened hair tore a sob from my throat. Too close, he was too close. I wasn't going to make it.

The vehicle skidded to a stop and two men burst from the vehicle with guns drawn.

Hardy and Quinn.

I fell to my knees on the concrete, screaming my relief.

Hardy's jaw was tight, his sapphire blue eyes glacial as he stared at my pursuer. "One more move, and I'll drop you where you stand," he roared through the quiet night.

Quinn flicked a glance at him, lips tight as he glanced at me. "You okay, Dakota?"

I nodded, once, sharp. I was alive. That's all that mattered.

Three police vehicles screamed to a stop a moment later.

It was finally over.

KRISTY AND DAVID BRAUER got extra charges slapped on top of the murder charges for their part in my kidnapping. They thought if they could silence me, this entire thing would go away. Nick sang like a bird when questioned and admitted to his role in everything, including the payments he accepted for his silence and the additional payment he accepted to 'take care of me' as he put it.

I rode home in silence. Hardy had wrapped me in a warm blanket and doctored my feet with a first aid kit Quinn kept in his vehicle.

"We can reschedule tomorrow," he said when we were almost home.

I straightened. "Absolutely not. You are marching down that aisle tomorrow whether you like it or not."

Hardy blinked. "Dakota. I'm not under duress, but you just went through something most people will never experience. Don't you want some time to deal with it?"

"I want to marry you more," I said mulishly. "I'm okay. We're all okay. Everything is planned. I'm not backing out of my wedding unless you want to."

Hardy slowly shook his head. "I didn't say backing out. I'd never back out."

"Then we're getting married tomorrow," I said quietly.

Hardy pulled me closer and pressed a kiss to my temple. "I'll marry you right now, Dakota. Never doubt that."

"Tomorrow is good enough," I said.

EPILOGUE

The wedding went off without a hitch despite the slight limp I had coming down the aisle. I must have tweaked a muscle in my mad dash to freedom last night, but it was nothing some muscle relaxers and a heating pad couldn't fix later.

Hardy's eyes held a shadow, but when he saw the doors open and I stepped into the aisle, the love his face held took my breath away.

It was a simple affair, just like we wanted, but everyone we cared about was there, and we had enough food to feed an army.

When we said our vows and sealed our union with a kiss under the stained-glass windows of the chapel, something inside of me uncurled and bloomed.

This was what it all came down to. Me and Hardy. Finally together for the rest of our lives.

And as a bonus, we got an adorable little dark-haired girl in the deal, too.

She hurled herself at us, and Hardy scooped her up in one arm as we headed out of the chapel and to the reception.

When we got into the car, the driver cranked the heat on. I buckled Izzy in, but before I could pull back, she took my face in her hands and studied me.

I held still, allowing her to stare. "Everything okay, Izzy?"

"I want you to be my mommy."

The words made my heart stutter. I pressed my palm against her hand and smiled. "I am your mommy, darling. You can call me Dakota for as long as you like, but if you ever want to call me Mom, I would love that more than anything."

Izzy looked at her dad who sat motionless beside me, holding his breath as he watched his daughter finally loosen the last of the knots around her heart, and nodded to herself.

"I want to call you that now."

A tear slipped down my face. "Then by all means, Izzy." I pressed a kiss to her forehead and inhaled her sweet scent. "I love you so very much."

"I love you, too."

And with that, we were off, heading toward the reception for a short celebration before we got down to the business of the rest of our lives.

. . .

THREE MONTHS LATER, Fletcher and I sat on the beach chairs gazing out at an azure, blue ocean. "Where to next?" she asked.

"We're talking about Europe." I sipped from the fluted glass the server had brought me earlier. Hardy and Cole were off golfing, and Izzy and Mom had elected to stay and use the swimming pool.

Fletcher wasn't supposed to be here, but during the reception she and Hardy got to talking and she revealed she held two master's degrees—one in early childhood education and the other in counseling. I knew the woman was intelligent, but I had no idea just how bright she was.

Hardy probed and realized while Fletcher loved being a journalist, she was itching to do something else. When he dangled an all-expenses paid trip to come and tutor Izzy and hang out with me on her downtime, Fletcher threw caution to the wind and readily accepted.

Cole was only here for a few days, and here more for Fletcher than us, but none of us minded.

Quinn checked in every few days, but things at home were running smoothly. He loved running the firm and so far, there had been zero issues—just a sharp rise in profit. The man literally did not care that we'd run off to explore the world, and I had to admit, I didn't miss the firm as much as I thought I would.

Hardy and I were discussing what to do next—whether we wanted to work something out long-term with Quinn or whether to sign most of it over to him while we figured out what we wanted to do with the rest of our lives.

For now, though, Fletcher and I were sunning our buns in the sun. Izzy was happy as a clam and had taken on the dark golden tan of a long-term sun worshipper, and Hardy looked more relaxed than I'd ever seen him.

Not a single mystery had unveiled itself to us, and I, surprisingly enough, had not gone looking for one either.

For now, I had all the mystery I needed wrapped up in a six foot plus hunk of a husband and a mischievous dark-haired little girl who'd squirreled away a part of my heart forever.

I smiled and let out a deep, content sigh.

Mysteries could stay buried for a little while longer.

They'd still be there when I got home.

ALSO BY S.E. BABIN

A Shelf Indulgence Cozy Mystery Series

How about a ghost whisperer in a new magical town? Check out
The Psychic Cleaner series!

Psychic Cleaner

Like a little more magic with your cozies? Check out The
Magical Soapmaker Mysteries!

The Magical Soapmaker Mysteries

If you'd like a little more action and sass and don't mind some
PG-13 language, check out my Aphrodite series.

The Goddess Chronicles

Or, if you like a snarky bartender with a secretive mixed heritage,
meet Violet!

Cocktails in Hell

ABOUT THE AUTHOR

Sheryl likes cake too much and can be found hoarding it while hiding from her children in the pantry closet.

Follow her on Amazon at: https://www.amazon.com/S-E-Babin/e/B00J1J236A

www.ingramcontent.com/pod-product-compliance
Ingram Content Group UK Ltd.
Pitfield, Milton Keynes, MK11 3LW, UK
UKHW041927310325
456929UK00002B/234